LJ BURKHART

The Fire Inside Me

A Fire Novel

First edition

This book was professionally typeset on Reedsy.
Find out more at reedsy.com

Contents

Chapter 1 1
Chapter 2 9
Chapter 3 19
Chapter 4 25
Chapter 5 35
Chapter 6 43
Chapter 7 50
Chapter 8 55
Chapter 9 61
Chapter 10 73
Chapter 11 81
Chapter 12 88
Chapter 13 98
Chapter 14 105
Chapter 15 111
Chapter 16 118
Chapter 17 127
Chapter 18 138
Chapter 19 145
Chapter 20 152
Chapter 21 158
Chapter 22 172
Chapter 23 180
Chapter 24 187

Epilogue 191
Author Notes 196
Acknowledgments 197
About the Author 199
Also by LJ Burkhart 201

Chapter 1

Anna

Yoga was where I always found my mother. She would come to me as I lay in Savasana, and she would hug me and tell me that everything would be all right and that she was proud of me. I never knew if it was just my imagination, or if she really was there as I was meditating, the gaps between realms more open. Or at least we as humans were more open to them.

I missed her so much. I missed her every single day. No one in my current life knew, but I lost my mother when I was thirteen to breast cancer. They didn't catch it until it was too late. I remember watching her deteriorate fast. One day she was laughing and talking and walking around fine, and then the next she was in the hospital on her deathbed.

But with yoga, I could feel her, if only for a few minutes, and today was no different.

When I was content, I took one more deep breath and sat up, looking around my home yoga studio. I loved this space. I tried to do yoga every day, whether it be a class or here on my own, depending on the day. I took another drink of water as I stood up and made my way down to my bathroom for a shower so I could start getting ready for work. I didn't need to wash my hair since I did it the day before, so I piled my ashy blond, almost white-gray locks on top of my head in a messy bun before undressing.

I turned the shower on and looked at myself in the mirror while I waited for the water to heat up. My bangs were too short to go in with the bun so they lay, sweeping across my forehead. My blue almond-shaped eyes were framed by dominant dark eyebrows that had a fairly dramatic arch and a barbell through the left one. My ears had multiple piercings in each, and I also had a stud in my small, slightly upturned nose and a ring through my full bottom lip.

My gaze worked its way down my body. I'd always had curves ever since I hit puberty, and it had always attracted attention, particularly of the male sort. I decided long ago that I would use that asset to my advantage whenever possible. It would be my weapon, not my weakness.

My full breasts were also pierced at my nipples(yes, I knew I had an addiction), my dark pink heart-shaped areolas (which were tattooed on) stood out against my fair skin. Something else my friends didn't know about me was that I got my tits chopped off when I was eighteen. When I got my first lady checkup, the doctor notified me that with my mother's history of breast cancer and the blood work I had done, it was likely I would get breast cancer just like her. I could've waited until I actually got cancer, but I hadn't wanted to go that route. So instead, I chopped 'em off, got a boob job, and got them tattooed. They were roughly the same size as mine were originally, maybe slightly bigger. They were 34D and they were 34C before my surgery. I didn't have many tattoos, just my nipples, a big t-rex on my thigh, the *Super Mario* star behind my right ear, the word *fight* on my left wrist, and some black henna-style tattoos on my fingers on both hands. Mostly moons and swirly things. I liked tattoos, but piercings were my thing. I also made sure to always get my nails done. Recently, I was loving the pointed, almost witch-looking nails, and they were currently black.

My eyes continued down, taking in my flat stomach with my double belly button piercing, and my wide hips with dermals on the insides of both hip bones. I did not, however, have my genitals pierced. I thought about it several times before deciding that it wasn't for me.

When my eyes went back to my face, I realized that the mirror was steamy. The water must have heated up a good amount while I was looking at myself. I stepped in, squealing at how hot the water was before readjusting the temperature. When it was comfortable, I settled in, relaxing in the spray as I thought about the day ahead of me. I would be seeing and talking to Savannah for the first time in a few days, which I was a little nervous about. I wasn't sure if Lauren had talked to her or not at all since I confessed my love for her. I'm sure Savannah wouldn't mind once she found out, but I really hoped that I hadn't completely fucked up our group dynamic. Even if Lauren hadn't told her, I probably would. I wanted my friend's advice.

I finished washing and got out. I turned my curler on before going to dress in my bedroom. My wardrobe mainly consisted of the color black, so I decided on tight black jeans with rips in the knees, a black T-shirt that had lace all along the back making it see-through, and black Toms. I quickly curled my hair and did my makeup, going with a subtle nude-beige palette. I sprayed a quick spritz of my signature perfume, Band of Outlaws, and I was ready to go.

Fifteen minutes later, I was walking into work. Savannah was usually always the first one here. She liked to be early, and she was fairly particular about how the shop was opened. She also always liked to have first dibs on music, and sure enough, as I walked in she had System of a Down blaring.

"Hey, bitch!" I yelled over the music.

Her face lit up when she saw me, and she quickly dashed over to the stereo to turn it down. "Hey! I've missed you around here. I feel like I haven't seen you in weeks."

"Oh, please. No one ever misses my crazy ass. And it's only been like less than a week."

"Yeah, well, maybe 'cause we haven't hung out in a while," she said. "I think we should try to have a girls' night with Lauren soon."

"Oh. I'm not sure she'll want to," I said, avoiding her gaze.

"Why? Did you guys get in another fight?" she asked.

"Not exactly."

"Okay. You need to tell me what the fuck happened. Usually you overshare and today you aren't giving me shit."

"Well, she came over the other day to tell me something and I might have told her that I was in love with her after I kissed her on the mouth…" I trailed off, getting quieter as I went, not wanting to tell her the rest, but knowing I needed to. Savannah didn't say anything for about thirty seconds. Her brows furrowed as she opened her mouth before closing it again, as if contemplating what to say.

"Well, honestly, about fucking time," she stated, shocking me like how I thought my statement would shock her.

"*What*?!" I screamed in my typical fashion. "You knew?"

"Of course I knew. I've seen the way you look at her. And then I really knew when you guys got into that huge fight. That had jealousy written all over it."

"Well, why didn't you tell me?"

"You needed to figure it out on your own," she said simply, shrugging.

"If you would've told me when you knew then you could've saved me a lot of shit," I grumbled, pissed that she saw it before I did.

"You wouldn't have listened to me and you know it."

"Oh, shut up, cunt," I said, elbowing her.

"So, what happened? What did she say?"

"I mean, overall it went pretty well. The first thing she said was 'I thought you said you'd only lick my pussy if I went into a fire and came out naked carrying three dragons.' We laughed a little awkwardly, and then I told her that that's what I thought too but I had been wrong. I explained to her that I discovered that was the real reason I had been upset with her. That I was glad she was with Phoenix because I wanted her to be happy, but my feelings for her had gotten in the way of that. She gave me a hug and told me that I was her best friend and she loved me too. She said that she was sorry she didn't feel the same way I did but that I would always be very special to her.

"After that she left and I haven't really talked to her since. I know we're technically okay, but I think things are going to be a little uncomfortable for a while. Especially if Phoenix is around. I don't know how he'll feel around me after all that."

"I'm sure he will be fine. Guys think lesbians are hot. He will probably just be upset that he wasn't there to witness it," she joked, making me laugh.

"Damn, you're starting to sound like me."

"Yeah, well, one of us needs to. I've missed your loudness and your inappropriate jokes."

"Yeah, I have too. I'll start to channel my obnoxious bitch again," I said. "So, have you heard anything more about Greg?" I asked. I felt like all we did lately was talk about Lauren and my drama.

"Nothing. I carry my gun with me everywhere I go just in case, and I've been going to the shooting range fairly regularly to make sure that I feel comfortable shooting, but he hasn't tried to make contact or anything. Obviously, I have my restraining order against him, but he's crazy enough that he won't give a shit about it. I know the other shoe is going to drop at some point, but for now I'm just living my life like normal."

"Absolutely. That's all you can do." I knew that better than anyone. I walked over to her and gave her a big hug, just as much for her as for me. "Everything will be all right, you'll see. And if not, you and I will have fun together in hell." She laughed and we broke apart.

The door opened then as one of the other tattoo artists came in and we both got to work setting up everything.

"What the fuck are we listening to?" Jordan asked as he started setting up his own station.

"Oh, fuck off, Jordy. First dibs. Maybe you should get here earlier than five minutes before we open next time and you can put on whatever the hell you want," I teased, punching him in the arm.

"You know that will never happen. You're lucky I'm even here before we open at all."

"I don't mind changing it for a while. What's your request, Jordan?" Savannah asked, being the polite one.

"Way to make me look like a bitch, Savannah!"

"Oh, please. You do that all on your own, baby," Jordan teased me back. "And put on some of the Roots."

"Well, at least you picked something good," I said.

Savannah's client walked in then and Jordan's client about ten minutes after. I had only one appointment that day, but piercings were different. I had a much bigger walk-in clientele than the tattoo artists, probably because it was a more spontaneous thing to get done since it wasn't permanent, so I wasn't worried. Still, I wasn't as busy as the other artists were so I typically did more of the reception duties. As soon as my station was set up, I went to the front desk and hung out, answering phone calls and surfing the internet.

My first walk-in came in at around noon. She had just turned eighteen and wanted to get her belly button pierced. No surprises there. Most younger girls wanted to get something pierced but didn't want their parents to see it, so they got it somewhere inconspicuous. When I got her in the chair, she looked terrified. Savannah was the type to calm down her nervous clients. I had heard her do it many times, but I wasn't one of them. She would figure out soon enough that it was no big deal.

Luckily, the setup for piercings was much quicker than for tattoos so she didn't need to get herself super worked up before it happened. I put gloves on and wiped down her belly with disinfectant before drawing my two little dots where the needle was going to go.

"Does that look okay for you?" I asked her to make sure she liked the spot. She looked in the mirror quickly before nodding at me and leaning back. I took the needle out of its package before looking up at her. "Ready?" She nodded again before looking up and away so she wouldn't have to watch, and I put the needle against her. "One, two..." I shoved the needle through before I got to three, knowing that she would've tensed up more. I heard her quick intake of breath before I followed the jewelry through after the needle.

"All right, you're all set," I said, wiping any blood from her skin before standing up and taking my gloves off.

"Thanks," she said, wiping stray tears from under her eyes. Piercings made people's eyes water a lot of the time.

We went up front and I charged her thirty dollars, expecting a shitty tip or none at all since she was only eighteen and looked a little privileged. Sure enough, she left the tip line blank as she signed her name at the bottom. I hoped that her parents paid for the card and they would see where she was spending her money.

The rest of the day went by slowly. I pierced my one appointment that came in at three, and luckily she was older than my first, not nervous, down to earth, and left me a generous tip. She had several piercings already and ended up getting her septum done.

The only other people I had were a group of three sisters who all wanted their lips done in some fashion. One got snake bites, the second got a Marilyn Monroe, and the last got just a regular lip ring. They all tipped me very well too, and I was pleased with the outcome of my day. I went home that night feeling content.

I sat on the couch and thought about maybe going to a yoga class the next morning. It had been a while since I had gone to one, and I felt in the mood to be around other people. I decided to check the website, and as soon as I opened the schedule, I saw Lauren's name next to the 9:00 a.m. class. My heart was beating a little faster as I wondered what to do. I really loved her classes, and I wanted to see her to make sure that things were still the same between us, but I didn't want to make her uncomfortable.

Fuck it. I was going to go, I decided. The only way that we would move past any awkwardness was to go about things normally. Plus, it was me. I could defuse tension better than anyone I knew. I mean, usually it was when I wasn't involved in the awkwardness, but I was sure it would be fine, especially since things had ended well. But there was only one way to find out. I was going to that class.

Chapter 2

Anna

I walked into the class more nervous than I'd been in a long time. I realized once I was finished getting ready that morning that I put in way more effort than I normally did when I was just going to a yoga class. I did my hair in a beautiful Dutch braid, loosening it so it was nice and full. My makeup was gorgeous in a subtle "I woke up like this" way, making me look fresh and rested, even if I wasn't. Finally, I had on my best yoga clothes: tight black leggings that were three-quarter length and had crisscross fabric and ties on the outer sides at the bottom—they always reminded me of ballet slippers—and a dusty-rose V-neck top with barely there sleeves that exposed my belly. Normally I wore something else over this top when I was out in public, but not today, I thought.

I turned the corner to see Lauren at the front desk checking someone in. I hadn't seen her for two weeks and I had missed her. She hadn't noticed me yet, so I stood back a little, patiently waiting my turn. The studio smelled like what I had come to associate with Lauren. Before her classes, and sometimes after, she always burned sage and palo santo. She had constantly done it when she lived with me in my little studio as well, and it reminded me of that comfortable feeling whenever you're home.

Finally, the woman in front of me, a redhead with very long, full hair, grabbed her things and headed toward the locker room. That was all the attention I gave her though, because in the next instant, I was locking eyes with the woman I was in love with. The one who saw so much of me, but didn't feel the same way. The woman who broke my heart but showed me who I was. There was so much said in the look we shared that it felt like an eternity, but in reality it was only a matter of seconds.

"Hey, sexy," I said. Probably not the best opener, since it was a reminder of our last encounter, but hey, I was awkward and had zero boundaries.

"Hey, hot stuff," she replied with a smile, making her way around the counter to wrap me in a tight hug. "I'm glad you came. I've missed you."

I sighed in relief that things hadn't changed between us and gave her a gentle squeeze. "I haven't come yet, but get me into a crazy position in class and I'm sure I will," I teased, smacking her ass as we broke apart.

"Oh, fuck off," she said, laughing. "Go put your stuff away and go into the studio."

"I haven't paid yet."

"Bitch, please. You know I never charge you."

"Is it because I'm so hot?" I asked, winking at her.

"Damn straight. Now get in there before people come in and steal your favorite spot."

I went to the locker room and set my stuff on the bench before taking my shoes and sweater off and putting them in a locker. As I was unzipping my yoga mat bag, I noticed the redhead from earlier. She was at the sink, washing her hands. I could see her face in the mirror, and I couldn't help staring at her. She was breathtaking. Her hair came down to the small of her back; it was wavy and full. I could tell that it was naturally red because it didn't have that fake tint to it, and her eyebrows were the same shade. Her skin was very light, lighter than mine, which was saying something, and she had nice full pink lips. Her light brown eyes met mine in the mirror and I quickly looked away, making myself busy with my yoga mat.

"Sorry, can I squeeze in here?" I looked up to find her standing next to me, gesturing to get behind me. "I forgot to put my shoes in my locker."

"Oh, of course," I said, stepping back. I felt her arm brush against mine and I inhaled sharply at the contact. I could also smell her as she passed, and I had to keep myself from visibly sniffing her. She smelled like amber and ginger. I had, of course, unknowingly chosen the locker right next to hers, so we were in close proximity to each other while I finally finished getting my stupid mat out of the fucking bag. I put the bag in the locker, grabbed my water bottle and mat, and went into the studio.

No one was in the room yet, which was my favorite. I liked having the space empty while I got into the zone. Not to mention that I had first dibs on placement. I always like the spot in front, in the corner. There was a mirror in front of me, and a mirror immediately to my right. That way I was always able to see my form and adjust accordingly.

I set up my black lotus yoga mat. This thing was awesome. It was a different material than most generic ones, which allowed me to hold my poses easier. A lot of mats were pretty slippery, especially when you were in a vinyasa class where you were sweating a lot, and when you had to hold down dog for a while. This one was really sticky, so I never had any problems with either of those. I also grabbed a blanket for me to sit on and use under my knees if I needed to. My last prop was a block, which I set next to my mat just in case I needed support in a pose.

Once I had everything how I wanted it, I sat on the blanket in the middle of my mat, cross-legged, and closed my eyes, getting into the mood while I waited for the class to start. I heard a few other people come in and set up, but I stayed still, even though sometimes it was hard for me not to look around.

Lauren came in sometime later, greeting us as she walked to the front. I opened my eyes to find that the redhead from earlier was almost directly behind me, and she locked eyes with me in the mirror before Lauren started her spiel. Whatever she said, I didn't even hear. The only thing I could see or pay attention to was the woman behind me. Every second that passed between us, the more heated our gaze became.

"So, on that note, let's everyone start in child's pose," Lauren said, breaking our connection. I shook my head to clear it before moving my blanket and situating myself comfortably.

As I lay there, I wondered what the hell was happening. I'd never experienced anything like this before. Even with Lauren, I didn't even start developing feelings for her until we had lived together for a little while. But with the woman behind me, it was like I felt instantly connected to her. It wasn't just an attraction, I mean that was definitely there too, but there was something deeper. Like she could see into my soul. Maybe we knew each other in a past life.

I decided to try to put her out of my mind for now so I could concentrate on my practice. It was harder than I anticipated. I could feel her eyes boring into my back as we moved, and I could feel myself showing off for her slightly. It was hard to keep the ego in check in yoga anyway, but put a hot girl behind me and it was impossible.

About halfway through, I felt myself slipping and my gaze kept wandering to her, especially in poses where I was already looking in her direction. She had a fantastic body. She was thin, but not overly so. She had a nice, firm round ass and small perky tits. I could tell that she had a lean, muscular body, and I guessed she was fairly religious about working out. She also had on an olive green tank top, which allowed me to see that she had a tattoo on her chest. From where I stood, it looked like a feather, but I couldn't be sure. My mind started wandering to where else she might have tattoos.

"Anna, rotate this hip to the left slightly." Lauren startled me from my thoughts by whispering to me and putting her hands on my hips, guiding them to the position they needed to be in. I adjusted accordingly, grateful to her for bringing my mind back to it. I took some deep breaths, refocusing myself.

Finally, after an extremely long class, Lauren guided us to Savasana. Even as I lay there, in my favorite pose, I didn't feel like I normally did. I was not able to meditate like normal; my mind was too distracted. I felt giddy about the end of class, as well as slightly nervous. Would the redhead talk to me? Should I talk to her? Would she brush up against me again to get to her locker? With all these thoughts running through my head, it was hard for me to lie still, and it felt like an eternity before Lauren finally called us out of the pose.

Normally after class, I stayed here, lying on my mat for about ten minutes. That day, I was almost the first one out the door. I bypassed the front desk, completely ignoring Lauren, which is also something I never did, to go straight to my locker. I would probably need to linger a bit in front of it, but I didn't want the redhead to leave before I could interact with her again.

I went to the sink and washed my hands, looking at myself in the mirror. I was a little sweaty from class and I had a few stray baby hairs coming out of my braid, but other than that I looked pretty good. When I was done washing my hands, I smoothed my hair with my wet fingers, taking care of the flyaways. I dried my hands and went back to my locker. A few women started coming in, and I made myself busy putting my yoga mat back into my bag to make it look like I wasn't waiting there for her.

A minute later, she gently touched my back before saying softly, "Can I squeeze by you again?" I silently moved backward, goosebumps rising on my skin, and I couldn't find my voice, something that was very un-Anna-like. "Great class, huh?" she asked, looking at me expectantly.

"Oh…yeah. The class was great," I repeated like an idiot. I was about to follow it up with something a little more dignified, but then she reached down and grabbed the hem of her shirt, lifting it over her head to expose a beautifully toned stomach. All concept of thought flew right from my head, and all I could do was stare at her. I blinked a few times and that cleared my head enough to get me to realize that I was still staring at her and she would probably get freaked out soon. I looked away at the perfect time, because in the next second I saw her doing the same thing with her tight sports bra. It took all my effort to keep my eyes focused on my stuff in the locker in front of me, and not on the gorgeous perky breasts that I could see in my peripheral vision. She also took off her pants and underwear before shoving all her clothes in her locker and grabbing a towel and wrapping it around herself.

She walked in front of me again, this time not having to ask or gesture since I hadn't moved since she came in, and went over to the shower area without another word to me. Well, I couldn't leave yet. I hadn't gotten her name or anything. All I'd managed to do was to make myself sound like a moron and gawk at her. Maybe I should take a shower too, I thought. That way, when she got out, maybe we would be alone in here and I could pull myself together enough to actually have a conversation with her.

I stripped quickly and turned on the shower next to hers. I tried to keep most of the water off my face and hair, while also listening closely for when her shower would turn off. As soon as I was done rinsing all the soap off my body, I heard the water cease in her stall. I quickly turned mine off as well, but as soon as I turned around to get out, I realized a horrible truth. I didn't have a towel. Oh God. I groaned out loud and cursed under my breath. I had no idea what to do.

"Excuse me, are you okay in there?" I heard her soft voice drift toward me on the other side of the curtain.

"Not exactly," I said, cursing myself and her body for making me so mindless. "I forgot that I didn't bring a towel with me," I said very quietly.

"Well, why don't you come on out and you can use mine. I just need to dry off and then you can take it," she replied, sounding just as friendly and cheerful as before.

"Are…are you sure?" I asked hesitantly, peeking my head out from behind the curtain. She smiled at me as she nodded.

"There's no one else in here. It's just us, so you can come out."

I looked around, and sure enough, everyone else had cleared out. I took a deep breath and opened the curtain, dripping wet in more ways than one, and followed her back to our lockers.

She quickly dried off, her eyes drifting toward my naked body every few seconds and I felt myself become drenched. It seemed she liked looking at me as much as I liked looking at her. I could clearly see now that she did indeed have a feather tattooed on her chest, going from her shoulder cap down under her collarbone and ending at the top of her sternum.

When she was finished, she stood up straight and met my eyes as she handed me the towel. Our fingers brushed and I could feel electricity shoot between our hands. I heard her sharp intake of breath and knew she felt it too.

"Thanks," I said, although it came out as more of a husky whisper.

She nodded and her gaze boldly drifted down my body. I wasn't modest, but I fought the urge to cover myself. She stopped on my nipples and I could see the question in her eyes. Before she could ask, I turned from her and started drying off with her wet towel. I kept getting whiffs of her delicious scent and had to stop myself from holding it up to my face and inhaling. When I was done, I turned back around to find that she had been staring at my ass and I had caught her in the act. She didn't, however, seem at all ashamed. I handed the towel back to her before opening my locker. We both started dressing in silence, aware of each other, but not saying anything. When we were both fully clothed, I turned to her and decided to introduce myself.

"I'm Anna," I said.

"I know. I heard Lauren say your name in class," she replied, smiling at me. "My name is Molly." How fitting, with her red hair. And now that she had said more than a few words I thought I could hear just a hint of an Irish accent. Oh God. I was a sucker for accents.

"Well, it's nice to meet you, Molly." This was so weird. I felt like for the first time in a long time, I was timid and had no clue what to say. I was being very awkward, which I sometimes was, but it was usually from me telling an inappropriate joke or coming onto someone.

"Anna," she said, and I melted at the sound of my name on her tongue, "are you doing anything tonight? Want to go grab a drink with me?" she asked. My heart skipped a beat, but I was slightly confused.

"Oh. Umm..."

"Like on a date. I guess I should've clarified," she said, smiling.

"I'm not sure."

"I see. Do you already have a girlfriend?" she asked, and I was so taken aback that I just stared at her for a minute.

"What?"

"I'm sorry. I thought you were a lesbian. My bad."

"Well...I just...I think I like women..." I stumbled around my words, completely clueless how to respond.

"Oh. You aren't quite ready to date one yet. I get it. It can be a little confusing at first. That's okay. It was nice meeting you, Anna." She started grabbing her things and went for the door. It was crazy. It was like she saw things in me that I had only found out about very recently.

"Molly, wait. I'm sorry. This is all very new for me, but yes I would love to go out for a drink with you." She looked back at me skeptically, as if unsure if I was actually ready to go out with her or not. I smiled widely at her, despite feeling slightly embarrassed and out of my element. That seemed to reassure her because she nodded at me and returned my smile.

"Okay. I will be at Indulge at eight o'clock tonight. I hope to see you there, but if not, I'll understand." She reached out to grab my hand and I grasped hers. We did a slight intimate handshake before she brought my hand to her mouth, grazing her lips along my skin. Then, she dropped it and turned to walk out. I stood there completely flabbergasted. I got my shit together, both figuratively and literally, and walked out into the lobby.

"About damn time, bitch. I was just about to send in a search party," Lauren teased.

"Oh, shut up. It wasn't that long."

"Girl, you were in there for like forty minutes."

"What? Seriously?"

"Yeah. And I just saw Molly come out. What happened?"

"Well, to spare you the embarrassing details, I have a date tonight," I said, excitement creeping into my voice.

"Oh my God. Really? That's great! I didn't know she was a lesbian."

"Well, she apparently knew I was one. I guess it wasn't that big of a surprise after we both were staring at each other's naked bodies."

"Jesus Christ, Anna. Did you guys fuck in the locker room? I have to clean that shit up!" Lauren scolded.

"Bitch, please. I've never fooled around with a woman before, and the first time I'm doing that is not in the locker room of a yoga studio.

That's more like the second or third time."

"You sound like an innocent little virgin." She laughed.

"I basically am. I feel like one. I'm nervous, I don't know what to do or what to say or how to act. Guys are so different. I know exactly what to do, I know how to act to make them do what I want. But this is completely out of my comfort zone," I rambled, my voice rising by the second, my nerves getting the better of me.

Lauren walked in front of me and grabbed me by my shoulders. "Anna, calm the fuck down. Savannah and I will help you. Let's call her, we can go to lunch, and then we will help you get ready for your date, okay?"

Chapter 3

Anna

The girls and I decided to go to Sushi Hai for lunch. It was our favorite spot and it was close to the yoga studio. Lauren and I arrived first because we were closest. As soon as we sat down, she ordered us all our favorite caramel apple martinis, probably to calm my ass down. Savannah showed up twenty minutes later, and we ordered appetizers and our sushi before starting in with each other, knowing that we needed to order before we started talking or we'd never eat.

"So what's going on? I'm all for a spontaneous lunch, but I feel like this is girl help time," said Savannah.

"Anna has a date."

"So? That's not anything new."

"It is when it's a hot redheaded woman."

"Yes!" exclaimed Savannah, clearly excited that I was exploring this new version of myself.

"I feel so out of my league here," I admitted. "I just have no idea what to do or how to act. And, I don't know how you bitches are going to help me since none of us has ever been with a woman before."

"Okay," started Lauren, "the best thing about this is that we *are* women. We know exactly how we think and how we want to be treated on a date. I think that's the key to this. Just think of what you like and what you want and turn that around."

"I agree," Savannah chimed in. "We know what men want and like because we've had years to figure it out, but we already know women so it shouldn't be that hard to decide how to act and what to do."

This conversation was already making me feel better. I never would've thought of that on my own.

"Okay, yes," I said, nodding in agreement and understanding. "But still, what about the sexual stuff? I don't know how to go down on a woman."

"Just because you never have doesn't mean you don't know how. Think about it. Honestly, I feel like it'd be easier than sucking cock," Savannah said, shrugging.

Of course, our server chose that moment to drop off our appetizers, giving us all a strange look. We ordered another round of drinks before diving into our edamame and potstickers.

As our martinis came, Lauren took a big drink and a deep breath, looking slightly nervous.

"So, I have some news."

"Is this what you were going to tell me when you came over that day?" I asked and she nodded, but remained silent.

"Well, what is it, bitch?" Savannah asked.

"Phoenix and I got married," she said quietly, as if fearful of our reaction. Savannah and I both stared at her in silence. Her face was getting redder by the second. "Will one of you please say something?"

"You didn't think to invite us?" Savannah asked, agitated. I was grateful she said something, because I still didn't have the words. Plus, I didn't want to be the only one upset, especially after all the drama that happened between us recently.

"Well, honestly, it was a last-minute thing. We woke up one morning and just decided to go to City Hall. And as much as I love you guys, I did want it to just be the two of us. With everything that happened with Ryan, I didn't feel like having a wedding. I didn't want to go through the planning and all that. I just wanted a really special day with the man I love," she replied, slightly teary.

I looked at her and tamped down my jealousy and anger. If anyone deserved to find happiness, it was Lauren. She had been through so much shit, and I was glad that she found it, even if it wasn't with me. Besides, I'd known for a long time that she could never return my feelings, and in a way, telling her had given me the closure I needed to start getting past this. It might help too that I had a date tonight with a very gorgeous redhead, a voice whispered in my head.

"Congratulations, babe," I said, reaching over to give her a big hug. She looked slightly surprised before leaning in and returning it. "I understand wanting to have that private moment between you. I'm sure your viewpoint on weddings changed when Ryan passed, and that's not necessarily a bad thing."

"Do you at least have pictures?" Savannah asked, still slightly bitter, especially since she knew I wasn't going to be pissed with her.

"I do, actually! These girls who were at the courthouse got all excited when we came out and insisted on taking a shit ton of photos of us," she said, pulling out her phone with a big smile on her face, clearly excited that she could finally tell us all about her big day. It was then that I noticed the thin band on her ring finger. I grabbed her hand and brought it closer so I could get a good look at it. It was beautiful and simple. Just rose gold with black diamonds.

"It's gorgeous, Lauren," I told her.

"Thank you," she replied, smiling at me. "Phoenix picked it out all on his own. Which makes up for the fact that he originally just wanted to go to the courthouse in our regular clothes. I think I almost killed him with my stare."

She showed Savannah the ring before opening up the photo album and laying her phone on the table in front of us. We both gasped at how beautiful she looked, and whoever the girl was who took the pictures deserved mad props. They looked professionally done. It took us almost a half an hour to scroll through all the photos, that's how many there were, but being women, we loved looking at them all, especially since we couldn't be there ourselves.

"So are you guys going to go on a honeymoon?" I asked.

"I think so. We haven't decided where yet though. Right now our top two choices are between Ireland and Costa Rica."

"Well, you'll have a blast either way," said Savannah, speaking from experience since she got back from her own honeymoon not long ago. "We talked about Ireland too. I think we'll definitely go eventually, but Greece was at the top of my list and Charlie gave me what I wanted."

"You know what would be fun? If Nix and I went to Costa Rica on our honeymoon and then we all took a trip together to Ireland!"

I almost groaned out loud. This would be a total couples' trip and I would be the fifth wheel. The only one without a partner.

"That would be awesome! What do you think, Anna?" Savannah asked.

"Yeah. Sounds great." Maybe by the time we actually went I'd have a partner. All of a sudden, a vision popped into my head of me and Molly in Ireland. Different images were coming, us with the group in a pub, drinking and dancing, walking along the cliffs there, the two of us tangled in bedsheets in an old castle. If that were the case, I would be all for it.

We finished our lunch and drinks and headed back to my apartment. I had a few hours before I needed to start getting ready for the date, so we mostly just did what we did best, hung out and talked. When it was finally time for me to get ready, the girls poured me a glass of wine, since I was a little nervous, and I hopped in the shower. I came out in my robe and they had three outfit choices already laid out on the bed for me.

The first one was a pair of high-waisted black button pants with a flowy V-neck rose-gold blouse and heels. The second was a classic little black dress with a slit up one side and silver heels. The third was a yellow flowy knee-length dress with a black waist belt and black flats. I looked at all the options and discarded the black dress; it was too formal for where we were going. The other dress looked too casual, more like it was for a girls' lunch than for a first date. My choice made, I quickly dressed in the first option, inserted the front of the shirt in my pants in a French tuck, and pulled it out so it was slightly loose.

Lauren blow-dried my long blonde hair for me, making it full and voluminous, and curled the ends with the round brush, giving it a Lana Del Rey wave. Savannah meanwhile was working on my makeup. We decided to go with a metallic eyeshadow to match my blouse with a black cat eyeliner. She then put a darker lipstick on me, deciding to go bolder since we went with a light eyeshadow. It was a matte plum-red, which was perfect to hide the fact that I'd already been drinking wine.

"All right, bitch. I think that's as good as you're going to look. Which is fuckin' smokin', if I do say so myself," Savannah said, smacking my ass.

I looked in the mirror and silently agreed with her. I checked the time on my phone. It was only seven, so I still had a whole hour before I was supposed to meet up with her. The waiting was driving me nuts. I wish I could just go already. I sat and started jiggling my legs up and down, my anxiety setting in.

Lauren got me another glass of wine, and the slight burn helped just a bit. I took a few deep breaths as the girls started trying to engage me in conversation to distract me.

"So, do you think she'll want to come over after?" Savannah asked.

"Oh, shit. I didn't even think of that! I need to clean the apartment.

Now," I said, quickly getting up and almost spilling my wine all over my blouse in the process.

"Anna, calm down. It's pretty clean right now anyway," Lauren said.

"It's tidy-ish. It's not clean, Lauren. Plus, you lived here, you're used to it when it's messy."

"Okay. We will all start cleaning. We've got plenty of time to make it look good in case she comes over here after. But I swear to God, if you fuck up all our hard work, I'll kick your ass."

The three of us did a quick sweep of the apartment. I handled the bathroom, considering that most people hated cleaning bathrooms and I wasn't about to make them clean my toilet. Lauren did the kitchen since she knew where all the dishes and everything went, and Savannah got the living room and bedroom, which mostly just needed straightening.

Forty-five minutes later, the apartment looked spotless and we had some candles and incense burning to make it smell nice. I did a quick check in the mirror to make sure I didn't fuck up my hair or makeup, and then I put on a quick spritz of my favorite perfume. We blew out the candles in the apartment and I was ready to go.

The girls walked me out and each gave me a kiss on the cheek for good luck.

"Text us as soon as you can to tell us everything that happened," Savannah told me, Lauren nodding in agreement behind her.

"I will," I replied, hopping in my car and waving at them. "Here we go," I told myself, taking a deep breath and heading toward the bar.

Chapter 4

Molly

I got to Indulge at 7:45. I figured she wouldn't be here yet, but I was always early to everything. I sat down at a quiet table in the corner so that we could have some privacy. I had a view of the door from where I was sitting, so I would be able to see her as soon as she walked in. *If she walked in,* I thought. I still wasn't sure if she would show up or not.

The waiter came up to the table to take my order, a younger guy, twenty-three by my guess. As soon as he walked up, his eyes strayed to my chest, and I rolled my eyes. When he didn't say anything for several seconds, I snapped my fingers in front of me and his gaze immediately shot up to my face. He had the decency to look slightly ashamed.

"Yeah, hi. Can I get a glass of your house Cabernet?" I said testily. I hated men ogling me.

"Of course, miss," he replied, red in the face. He didn't even check my ID. I guess I couldn't blame him. My dress was very low cut in a V-neck fashion, it was olive green and sleeveless, and the waistband was slightly above my belly button. It was floor length but had slits on either side that came up to above my knees, and the back above the waistband was pretty much nonexistent. It only had straps connecting the shoulder piece to the bottom half of the dress, and another set that connected both of the sides together so that my boobs wouldn't fall out. I had paired a pair of nude strappy heels with it. I didn't wear this dress very often, but this was my favorite color so it made up most of my wardrobe. I always liked the way it looked with my red-orange hair, which was falling around my face in long, big waves.

The server came back a minute later with my wine. As he set it down in front of me he asked me if I needed a food menu. I told him I would take one just in case. I didn't know if she would be hungry when she got here. *If she got here,* I reminded myself again.

I normally didn't go out with newbies, but there was something about Anna that I couldn't explain. I knew she felt it too; I could tell by the way that she reacted to me and looked at me. I, in turn, was surprised by my own reaction. I couldn't stop staring at her in that yoga class. It didn't help that her round, delicious ass was bending over in front of my face for a whole hour, not to mention that her outfit had left little to the imagination. And then, she had walked out of that shower as naked as the day she was born, with the exception of the multiple piercings she had gracing her body.

I couldn't stop my eyes from taking their fill of her. I had almost asked about her nipples, but when she turned away from me, I assumed that she had noticed and didn't want me to mention it. That was fine. If tonight went well, I'm sure I'd find out eventually. I could feel myself growing wet thinking about her naked body, and about all that might happen tonight. Then again, if she was just coming out she might not be ready for too much physical contact yet. That could be fun in and of itself.

I heard the front door open, and I looked up just in time to see her walk in. She looked absolutely gorgeous. I smiled, waving at her to get her attention. Her eyes locked on mine and a dazzling smile lit her face before she made her way over to me.

"Hi," she said breathlessly.

I stood up and wrapped her in a hug, "Hey, siúcra," I replied, the nickname sliding off my tongue naturally. The hug lasted longer than anticipated. Her body felt so nice against mine, warm and inviting.

We pulled away and sat down across from each other. The waiter came up again, this time his eyes wandered over Anna's body, and I cleared my throat, irritated that he was now eyeing my date. He quickly glanced at me, smiling sheepishly before asking Anna what she'd like to drink.

"Can I try yours?" she asked me.

"Of course." I held my glass out for her and our fingers touched as she took it from me. Her lips brushed the glass and I watched her delicate throat swallow the dark liquid.

"I'll have a big glass of this, please," she said, handing my glass back to me. The server scurried off and I had a hard time not glaring at him. Anna seemed to notice because the next moment she was asking me, "What's wrong?"

"Oh, nothing. He just has a hard time keeping his eyes to himself. He was staring at my tits for about ten seconds when I first got here, and now he's staring at you too."

"Well, I don't blame him. Your breasts look good enough to eat. Or maybe just to eat off of," she stated matter-of-factly, her own gaze drifting down to my cleavage. I almost choked on my wine, I was so surprised that came out of her mouth.

"Too much? Sorry. I have no filter, and it's worse when I'm nervous."

I laughed and blushed, which happened often and was unfortunately easy to notice because of my fair complexion.

"Don't be sorry. You just caught me off guard. It's nice to know that you'd like to eat off of them. Maybe we can try that later." She laughed, sounding relieved that I wasn't offended. "Speaking of eating, are you hungry?"

"Yes. I'm starving, actually."

I handed her a menu and we were both silent as we perused the food options. A minute later, the server dropped off Anna's wine, and we told him we were ready to order. It seemed like he was having an awfully hard time concentrating and he kept blinking, almost like he was trying to prevent his eyes from moving downward.

"I'll have the filet mignon, medium rare," Anna said.

"That comes with mashed potatoes and veggies, is that okay?"

"Sounds delicious."

"And for you, miss?" he asked, turning to me.

"I'll have the Mediterranean flatbread," I answered. As if on cue, his eyes once again made their way to my breasts. Before I could say anything, Anna chimed in.

"Oh, and by the way"—she looked down at his name tag—"Derek, neither of us are interested in men, and we happen to be on a date, so could you keep your eyes on our faces, please? Thanks," she said in a sweet voice with an even sweeter smile as she handed him the menus. He blinked, clearly as surprised as I was that she said anything.

"I'm so sorry, ladies. It won't happen again," he stammered before taking off toward the kitchens. I laughed loudly, deciding that I really liked Anna's style.

"How much you wanna bet that he'll be staring at us more now that he knows?" she asked me.

"Oh, that will definitely be the case, but my guess is that it will be at a distance now. He will also be telling all of the other servers, so don't be surprised if we get random workers walking by our table."

As if on cue, a group of waiters stuck their heads out of the kitchen and glanced in our direction. We both laughed loudly and Anna waved at them.

"I'm glad you decided to come tonight. I wasn't sure if you would or not," I told her.

"Well, how could I turn down such a sexy woman?"

"You seemed close for a minute there," I replied, her comment making me blush again.

"That had nothing to do with you."

"Yeah, I know. That's why I'm surprised you're here. So, it's a recent discovery for you?"

She nodded, taking a drink of her wine, whether it was to get out of verbally answering me or just coincidental, I wasn't sure.

"Have you ever been with a woman before?"

It was her turn to blush. "No. I only figured it out about a month or two ago," she said quietly, which I had a feeling was unusual for her.

"Can I ask how it happened?"

"Well, I've always known I was somewhat attracted to women, but I thought that it was mostly appreciating their beauty. Then, my old roommate and best friend started seeing this guy and the more time they would spend together, the more jealous I got. At first I just thought that it was because she wasn't spending as much time with me, but then one day we got into this huge fight and I was very irrational about the whole thing. After it was over, it dawned on me that it was because I had feelings for her."

"I see. Have you told her how you felt?"

"Yes. About two weeks ago. I've known since I had the revelation that she didn't feel the same way. She's pretty much as straight as they come."

"Have you spoken to her since?" I asked.

"Well," she said uncomfortably, "yes, actually. It's Lauren. Our yoga teacher from this morning." She was looking down at her hands, which were twisting together on the table.

"Oh, I see," I said, trying to tamp down my irrational jealousy.

She seemed to pick up on it though, because she reached across the table to grab my hand. "She's married. She just told me today."

"And how do you feel about that?"

"Honestly, not nearly as bad as I thought I would. It finally feels like we're getting back to our old normal friendship. I think telling her how I felt a couple weeks ago and hearing from her own mouth that she didn't feel the same way really helped me to move on. Plus, I had a really hot date to look forward to tonight," she teased, winking at me.

I laughed and squeezed her hand. "So how do you feel about the prospect of being with a woman?"

"Well, I'm fucking nervous, but every time I think about you riding my face, moisture floods between my legs, so I'll take that to mean I'm also very excited."

I gasped at her words, blood flowing to both my face and my pussy. With her not being experienced in this field, I was not anticipating her being so blunt. I liked it.

"So you think you'd feel comfortable with that then?"

"How about we finish dinner and have some dessert, and then you can come over to my apartment and we will just play things by ear. I will tell you if things are moving too fast or if I don't feel comfortable with something, okay?"

"That sounds like a wonderful plan."

"Just…" she hesitated. "I just don't really know what I'm doing, so will you tell me if I'm not doing something right?"

I chuckled. "Siúcra, believe me, it will be way more natural than you think. I'm sure you won't need any guidance."

Just then, Derek came up to the table with our food. We also took that moment to order another round of drinks. I noticed that he kept his eyes firmly down, dropped off the food, and headed straight back to the kitchen, no doubt not wanting to be told off by Anna again.

"What do you keep calling me?" she asked a few minutes later while she cut up her steak.

"Siúcra. It means 'sugar' in Irish," I replied.

"I thought I could detect a hint of an accent. So you're Irish then?"

"Yes. I grew up in Cork. It's in the southwest part of the island. But we moved to the States when I was seven."

"Do you ever make it back there?" she asked.

"Yeah, we do. We still have extended family there so I would say we make a trip out like every three years."

"Do you speak Gaelic?"

"I do. But actually, that's not the native language there, though a lot of people assume that it is. Gaelic is actually Scottish, and Irish, or Gaeilge as we like to call it, is what we speak in Ireland, but I speak both." I could feel my accent getting heavier the more we talked about it.

"Wow. Maybe I'll have you talk dirty to me in Irish later," she flirted, a little breathlessly, and I smiled and raised my eyebrows knowingly at her.

"Want a bite?" Anna asked, holding out a piece of steak on her fork for me.

"Actually, I'm a vegetarian."

"Oh, sorry. I should've known since you have zero meat on your plate."

"It's no big deal. I'm not offended by it or anything, I just prefer not to have it. Especially red meat. I used to eat it, but my body really doesn't do well with it. Occasionally you might be able to persuade me to eat chicken or fish though."

"I see. That sucks. I love red meat. Do you have to take iron or anything?"

"Yeah. I take it daily, but I'm so used to it now that it doesn't even faze me."

"How long have you been a vegetarian?"

"About three years. I went to the doctor because I was having all sorts of stomach problems and she told me that I should try cutting out red meat. Sure enough, that's what it was."

"And how long have you been a lesbian? Or known, I guess I should say," she asked out of nowhere.

"Oh. Honestly, I've always known. Or at least when kids start liking other kids. I always thought boys were gross. I've never even been with a man. I kissed one once when I was in high school, but that's the only contact I've had."

"Wow. I'm a little jealous. I wish I would've figured it out a long time ago."

"Or maybe," I said softly, "you're finding out exactly when you should be."

She looked up at me and smiled. "Yeah, maybe I am."

We both were silent again and continued eating and drinking. When we were finished, I asked her if she still wanted dessert. We ordered a chocolate layer cake slice to split.

"So, what do you do?" she asked before it arrived.

"I'm an acupuncturist. I work at a community clinic."

"Oh, how cool! I've never had acupuncture, but I've always been tempted."

"I'd love to work on you sometime. What about you?"

"I'm a piercer. I work in a tattoo shop in town."

"How crazy that we both work with needles," I remarked.

"Yeah, that is strange. I love them. I know most people hate them, but I like the sharp bite. God, does that make me sound crazy? Or like a druggie? Jesus, Anna," she reprimanded herself, shaking her head. "I'm not, I swear."

I laughed. "Good to know. I understand though. I don't love them like you, but I don't mind them, especially with acupuncture. The needles are so small that you don't usually feel that same sting. It can sometimes be painful though, but in a very different way."

"Oh, really? How so?"

"Well, it's kind of hard to describe. It's more like a surge of energy, more like a zing instead of a sting, if that makes sense."

"Not really, but when I experience it, I'm sure it'll make perfect sense."

The cake showed up then, and we both dug in. When there was only one bite left, I picked it up with my fork and held it out to her. Her eyes met mine as she leaned forward and wrapped her lips around the fork, pulling the cake free and licking any crumbs from her mouth. Not able to resist the urge, I leaned forward, grabbed the back of her head, and pulled her to me.

Our lips met in a fevered passion. It was a quick kiss, since we were in public, but very heated. She tasted like chocolate and wine. It was sinful and I moaned into her mouth. Before we could get too carried away, I pulled away, sitting back into my seat once more. Her fingers came up to touch her own lips as if she couldn't believe what she felt, a dazed look on her face. I knew the feeling. I'd never had a kiss quite like that either.

When I looked away from her, I noticed our server, Derek, was standing next to the table staring with his mouth open, holding our check. He looked like he had just witnessed the most miraculous thing in the whole world. I cleared my throat and he quickly dropped the check on the table and scurried off. I looked at Anna and we both busted out laughing.

I snatched the bill and put my credit card in the envelope, ready to leave now that we had had some physical contact with each other. All I wanted to do was get her alone.

"Oh, you don't have to do that," she said, rummaging through her purse.

"You can get it next time, siúcra," I replied, winking at her. It was her turn to blush, but she smiled widely at me.

As soon as the check was paid for, we stood up and I grabbed her hand as we walked out front together. We got some looks from people as we passed, but I was so used to it that I barely even noticed it anymore. I got the sense that Anna was holding her tongue, and was tempted to make a spectacle just to shove it in their faces, but we made it outside without incident.

"So, would you like to come over?" she asked shyly.

"After that kiss? Hell yes."

She chuckled. "Okay, I'm in that car there," she said, pointing. "Why don't you follow me?" She then rattled off her phone number for me in case we got separated.

I hopped in my car and, with my heart pounding, followed her to her apartment.

Chapter 5

Anna

I tried not to drive too fast back to my place, but it was extremely difficult. My breathing was out of control and I was shaking slightly. I was excited that I would get to spend some alone time with Molly, but now that she wasn't right in front of me, I was so nervous.

That kiss was phenomenal. I had never felt anything like it before. Don't get me wrong, I had good kisses before, but nothing like that. Maybe because a woman had never kissed me? Or maybe it was specific to Molly.

Luckily, my apartment wasn't far from the bar, and we were parking our cars five minutes later. I closed my eyes and took a few slow, deep breaths to calm down before shutting my car off and getting out.

"You, my dear, have a lead foot," she teased as she met me on the sidewalk.

I laughed, my nerves lessening, and replied, "Well, I'm not usually that bad, but it didn't help knowing that I had a hot girl behind me."

"I know the feeling," she said in a low murmur, the teasing tone gone from her voice. She was inching closer to me, as though tempted to kiss me again.

"Let's head inside before the neighbors call the cops on us for getting naked in public," I said before she could touch me and rational thought left me.

She chuckled. "Good thinking. Lead the way." I walked in front of her and felt her hand at the small of my back, supporting me. Her touch was so different from what I was used to; it was delicate and gentle, just what I felt I needed.

We got up to the apartment door and I could feel her behind me. She brushed my hair to one side and leaned in to drag her lips along the side of my neck, her hot breath tickling me. I closed my eyes, relishing the contact, as I struggled with my keys.

"I'll never be able to get the door open with you doing that," I said breathlessly. She chuckled, and I could feel the vibrations against my skin.

"You can do it. I have faith in you, and you taste too good to stop."

I took a deep breath, opened my eyes, and focused really hard on my keys. After about thirty seconds, I got the door open, breathing a sigh of relief that we were inside. I set my bag down on the floor and turned to her. She had fire dancing in her eyes and I could see her nipples were pebbled under the thin fabric of her dress. I forced my gaze up to her face.

"Do you want more wine?" I asked, my voice husky.

"Yeah, I think that's a good plan," she said, smiling at me. It immediately put me at ease. I didn't want this to feel rushed, and my nerves were still present. I knew more wine would help me to relax. I went into the kitchen and opened one of the many bottles I had in here.

"This is a really nice apartment," Molly commented as she followed me in, glancing around appreciatively.

"Thanks. I loved it from the second I walked in. I've lived here for about five years now."

"What's up there?" she asked, pointing to the spiral staircase.

"Oh, that's my yoga studio."

"Really? Can I go look?"

"Of course," I replied, handing her a glass of wine and gesturing her forward. I grabbed my own before following her. I couldn't help but stare at the back of her dress. Her entire gorgeous back was exposed and right in front of my face. Without thinking, I reached my hand up to trail down her back. I heard her sharp intake of breath as I traced my fingertips along her spine, but she kept walking. Once we reached the top, she gasped again at the room.

"Oh, Anna, it's wonderful."

"Thanks. I love it too. I'm up here a lot."

She walked around the room, her fingers dragging over everything in sight, my stones, my tapestries, my yoga mat shelf with my little buddha on it. She inhaled deeply. "Sage?" she asked, and I nodded. "I can feel your energy strongly in here," she said, closing her eyes and breathing deeply. "This is where you let your walls down," she stated, not asked.

I held my breath, hardly believing what I was hearing. How could she know that? Was there other stuff that she could sense about me? Stuff that I'd buried deep down that no one knew?

She opened her eyes, and saw the look on my face. "I'm sorry, Anna. I didn't mean to freak you out. I just get a sense of energy sometimes, probably from what I do for work."

"It's okay. You didn't freak me out," I lied, trying to calm my racing heart.

"You don't need to lie, siúcra. I'll try to tone it down a bit. I will say, though, I've never felt an energy as strong as yours." She walked over to me and squeezed my hand, immediately putting me at ease. "Want to head back downstairs?" she asked, and I nodded again.

It was so strange. I never considered myself a shy or naive person, but with Molly, I definitely felt like that. I wasn't sure what it was about her, but I felt like she was seeing past my exterior to the part of myself that I never showed anyone. The person who was closest to seeing that part of me was Lauren, but even then, it was only the briefest glimpse. I shook my head to return to the present as we made our way back downstairs.

When we entered the kitchen I grasped her hand and pulled her into the living room with me. As she sat, I went around lighting candles. Luckily, my twinkle lights were always on so I didn't have to plug those in. Then, pulling a page from Savannah's book, I turned on some music, my Chillwave Pandora station. When there was nothing left for me to do, I grabbed my wine, and took a seat on the couch next to Molly.

"You don't need to be nervous, Anna. We can take this as slow as you want."

"I'm not nervous," I said too quickly.

Molly smiled at me, stroking her thumb down the side of my face. "What did I say about not having to lie to me?"

I chuckled before taking a deep breath and looking her in the eyes. "I am a little nervous, but I guess I feel like I shouldn't be. I'm not the scared little virgin type."

"Well, coming out kind of puts you right back in your teens. You are a virgin in a certain sense, and that's okay." Our bodies were moving closer to each other as she spoke.

"In any case, I'm not as innocent as you might think," I said quietly.

"Believe me, siúcra, I would never categorize you as innocent," she whispered, now a breath away.

Normally, I would've said some smart ass or sexy comment, but all thoughts flew from my head. With her this close, I could smell her amber perfume and the sweet wine on her lips, which made me lick my own. Also, under normal circumstances I was the aggressor, automatically taking control, but I didn't want to with her, so I stayed exactly where I was. Our eyes locked and I felt like I was in a kind of trance. I couldn't move or look away, or even breathe. She finally closed the gap between our mouths, and the spell was broken. I immediately wrapped my arms around her, my fingers tangling in her long hair and pulling her as close to me as possible. My breath started coming quickly, as if I couldn't get enough air or enough of her, I couldn't tell which.

The next moment I felt her pushing me against the back of the couch so that she could straddle me as she bit my bottom lip, sucking it into her mouth. I moaned at the delicious pain and moved my hips against hers. She pulled away a fraction, grasping my hair in one hand and locking our gazes again. She searched my eyes deeply and I noticed the barely restrained fire dancing behind hers. It was the same look that was there when she saw me naked in the locker room. She tilted my head to the side and softly bit down on my earlobe.

"Tell me you want this, Anna. That you want me," she whispered in my ear.

"Yes, Molly. I want you so badly I can hardly breathe. I've never felt like this before." The words tumbled out of my mouth, surprising me with their honesty and intensity.

To bring the point home, I reached up and skimmed my hands along the tops of her shoulders, gliding the straps of her dress down her arms. Within two seconds her breasts were exposed and my mouth watered with the thought of tasting her. I looked up into her eyes and she just sat there waiting for me to do whatever I wanted to her. She looked magnificent. Like a queen. When my attention wandered back to her chest, I noticed that she had goosebumps, and that her nipples were hard and staring me right in the face. I couldn't resist. I moved her hair out of the way and licked up the center of her sternum before making my way toward her left nipple. I took one taut bud into my mouth and sucked hard, making her draw in a sharp breath. Her fingers were already in my hair, hanging on for dear life. Her hips were subtly moving over mine, looking for any friction she could find.

I pulled back and blew the wet skin, making her shiver and more goosebumps appear, before I moved to give the other equal attention. When I had her thoroughly worked up, I gently bit down, scraping my teeth against her right breast as I pinched her other nipple between my thumb and forefinger. She gave out a little squeal and then a long, low moan.

"Are you sure you've never done this before?" she asked me, slightly breathless. I chuckled, but I didn't answer since my mouth was still working over her chest. After another few minutes, she pulled my head back and attacked my lips with her own. If our last kiss was heated, this one was as hot as hell itself. Her fingers drifted to my shirt and lifted it away from me, breaking away only when it reached where we were connected. She then made quick work of my black lace bra.

Her gaze drifted to my torso. I knew the question was on her tongue, but instead of asking it like I thought she would, she situated us so I was lying flat with her over me. Her mouth then began to worship me, her tongue dragging over every inch of exposed skin she could find. Before I knew it, I was a writhing mess. When she got to my stomach, she nipped along the waistline of my pants, her fingers reaching for the buttons. She paused and looked up at me, and I nodded enthusiastically. I did not want her to stop. She unbuttoned them and I lifted my hips to help her. We had a moment where we couldn't get my tight-ass pants off and we took a second to laugh, but we got them off in the end.

And then, I was lying there, with only my black lace panties to cover me from her gaze. I reached up and pushed her dress the rest of the way off of her, not wanting to be the only one bared. I was pleasantly surprised to see that she hadn't been wearing anything under it. I looked up at her, my gaze questioning. She chuckled.

"I hate wearing underwear of any sort, and only do it when I absolutely have to."

I groaned at her words.

"I will never look at you fully clothed the same way again. Especially in a dress."

By this time she was back to worshipping my body with her mouth. Her hands were also anywhere they could touch, dragging over every inch of me. Her lips whispered along my panty line and I shivered. She went back and forth multiple times before venturing lower. I could feel her nose run along my slit and I bit my lip in anticipation. I heard her inhale deeply before she moaned, her breath tickling and warming me.

"Fuck, siúcra. You smell heavenly," Molly groaned.

My breath hitched as her fingers hooked beneath my panties and slowly dragged them down my legs. She sat up, her hands moving to my knees and spreading them wide. Her fingers gripped my knees tighter as she straight up stared at me for a solid thirty seconds. I could feel wetness dripping between my lips and traveling toward my asshole, and by this time I was panting. The anticipation was excruciatingly wonderful, it was making me more excited and more nervous with every passing second.

Finally, she took her thumb and gathered the moisture that had slipped from my body before spreading it around my lips and my clit. At the first touch I moaned loudly, not able to stop myself. It felt exquisite and soon she had her whole hand involved. I wasn't even sure what she was doing, but I had never felt anything like it before. She was exploring every inch of my pussy with her fingers, and before I knew it, I was completely drenched and every drop from my body was spread around. She still hadn't touched inside of me though, and I wanted her to so badly. There were a few times where she got close, but I think she knew what I wanted but wasn't giving it to me yet.

"Please, Molly," I begged, unable to stop myself.

"What do you want?" she asked me, even though she knew.

"Your fingers inside of me," I whimpered.

She gave me a smug smile as she took just her pointer finger and slowly inserted it into my body. She was teasing me, but I didn't care, she had given me exactly what I asked for. I immediately moved my hips down hard and fast, impaling myself on her hand. I knew I had taken her by surprise, but I was too far gone to be ashamed. My hips moved shamelessly up and down, taking what I so desperately wanted from her. I felt a moment of pressure, and I could tell she added another finger into the mix, maybe two.

"Do you like fucking my hand? You're using it as a sex toy, you greedy little thing," she cooed at me, making me high off of her words.

"Yes, more, please" was all I could get out between pants.

Next thing I knew, her lips were closing around my clit and sucking it into her mouth. I let out a scream at the pleasure of it, and gripped her hair tightly in both of my hands. I might have been on the bottom but that didn't stop me from moving. I was fucking her hand and mouth with all I had in me. I could feel her moans vibrating against me, and I knew she liked how much I was responding to her. Her tongue ventured down both sides of my lips and while it wasn't as intense as my clit, it built me up slowly, the fire seeping into my veins at a maddening pace.

When she finally moved back to my hotspot, I felt like I would drown in the pleasure. It was overflowing, and I knew it wouldn't be long before I exploded.

"Molly, I'm close."

"Yes, siúcra. Come all over me," she groaned against my body.

With her words, I tumbled over the edge into the most intense and wonderful orgasm of my life.

Chapter 6

Molly

I could feel Anna's orgasm clutching my fingers as her wetness dripped from her. I lapped it all up and then crawled up her body, before kissing her with all the built-up tension inside of me, letting her taste how delicious she was. She kissed me back with equal passion, and the heat in my pussy reached a breaking point. I really wanted her mouth and hands on me, but I didn't want to push her too fast.

I lay on top of her as our lips and tongues continued their frenzied battle. I could feel her heart hammering against my chest, and I wondered if she was still nervous or if it was left over from her orgasm. Before I could put too much thought into it, I felt her hands wandering from my bare back around to my breasts. She cupped the weight of them in her palms, her thumbs gliding back and forth, and making my nipples peak. She pulled her mouth from mine and looked up into my eyes.

"Sit on my face," she breathed, and I could tell the thought of it both terrified and thrilled her.

"Are you sure you're ready, siúcra?"

"Yes. I want to."

Not needing any more prompting, I climbed up and situated myself above her. Her hands found my breasts once more and she pinched my nipples hard before gliding her hands down my torso. Once they reached the apex of my thighs, she spread me wide open. I could feel the air teasing my clit and I squirmed, even though she had hardly done anything to me yet. She turned her head and gently bit down on my thigh, before soothing away the hurt with her tongue. She did the same thing to my other leg, and then she started kissing a trail to my pussy. When she finally got there, she grasped my ass with both hands, and pulled my body down onto her face, her lips latching on to my clit with hard suction. I gasped in surprise and pleasure, but it quickly turned into a loud moan. I could feel her groan of appreciation vibrate against me and it only excited me more.

"Ride me, Molly," she said against my skin, making me moan again.

I planted my knees firmly on either side of her head and did what she told me. Her tongue felt phenomenal. If I hadn't known that she had never been with a woman, I would have guessed that she had done this a million times.

"Touch yourself, Anna. I want you to come again with me," I breathed.

I could hear her following my instructions, and my movements over her became more frenzied. I couldn't believe I was already this close to coming. I grasped her hair with both hands and held her in place as I rode her face hard. Her tongue glided through my folds and plunged into my cunt with every thrust. Her other hand reached up and grasped my nipple tightly between her fingers, giving me an unrelenting, painful pleasure.

"Anna, I'm close. Come with me."

I felt the movements of her hand that was between her legs become faster. Just as I was about to go over the edge, I heard and felt her wail of pleasure, and it pushed me into my own wonderful bliss.

She continued to lick me until I sagged against her, the remnants of my orgasm fluttering delightfully through my body. I moved off of her face and lay down next to her on the couch. She immediately snuggled up against me, letting out a little sigh of satisfaction.

"So, was it everything you thought it would be?" I asked, curious how her first experience was.

"My fantasy didn't even come close to that. I had no idea it could be like this," she said quietly.

"Well, honestly, it's never been that intense for me either."

Her head popped up as she stared into my eyes, hers full of surprise. "Really?"

"Really."

She smiled, giving me a soft, sweet kiss before lying her head back on my shoulder as I stroked my finger up and down her arm. We stayed like that for the longest time, just listening to the music and each other's breathing. My eyes drifted toward her chest, and the question I so desperately wanted to ask was on the tip of my tongue again.

"Anna...?"

"Huh?" she replied sleepily.

"Can...well, can I ask about your...breasts?" I asked quietly, and felt her tense against me. I immediately regretted it. "Never mind. I shouldn't have asked."

"No, it's okay. I just haven't ever told anyone about it."

"Not even Lauren?"

"Nope. Not even her. There's a lot that I haven't told anyone." I felt her take a deep breath and heard her swallow loudly. "My mother died of breast cancer when I was thirteen. The doctors all thought that I would get it too, so instead of waiting for the cancer to invade, I got them removed when I was eighteen. I didn't want to go through what my mom did. I still get tested every year just to be safe, but after I got the surgery they've never found anything."

"Oh, Anna. I'm so sorry." My voice broke on my last word. I kissed her forehead and held her closer to me. There was of course nothing I could say, but I could give her comfort.

"Thanks. I miss her a lot. She was an extraordinary person." Her voice didn't crack at all, but I thought I felt a tear glide down my chest. "Will you spend the night?" she asked, and I could hear the vulnerability in her voice.

"Of course, siúcra. I was hoping you wouldn't toss me out after you had your wicked way with me," I teased her, and she chuckled.

She stood up, grabbed my hand, and pulled me toward the bedroom. We didn't bother grabbing our clothes. We climbed into her bed and she turned her little TV on, putting on an old movie to go to sleep to. I had the feeling this was her nightly routine. We cuddled up naked next to each other, watching *Gone with the Wind* until we both fell asleep.

I woke to hear Anna moaning in her sleep. And not in a good way. I could feel the sheets sticking to me because of the sweat from her body.

"Anna," I said softly, trying to wake her without startling her.

"No…" she moaned again.

I clutched her to me and petted her hair, rocking her and saying as gently as I could, "Anna, sweetie. Wake up, it's just a bad dream."

After a minute or so she woke up, breathing heavily. She jerked away from me before her eyes focused on mine.

"Molly?"

"Yeah, it's just me, siúcra." I opened my arms for her to cuddle up to me again. She did immediately, and I felt her heart beating hard against me, her fast breathing tickling my chest.

"Wanna talk about it?" I asked, and she shook her head. "Do you want your movie back on?"

She nodded her head this time, and my heart broke for her. She was reminding me of a scared little kid, and I hated to see her so vulnerable. I turned the TV back on and got up to go to the bathroom.

While I was up, I got her a glass of milk. It's always what my mam would do when I had a bad dream or couldn't sleep. I gave it to her and then went to her dresser, finding comfy clothes for us both. When we were both fully clothed and she had finished her milk, we climbed back into bed. Ten minutes later we were sleeping soundly once more.

I woke the next morning with Anna draped around me like a vine. As much as I loved it, I was too hot, especially in all these clothes. I gently tried to extract myself from her, but as soon as I moved, she was awake.

"Good morning, sunshine," I said, smiling at her.

"Good morning," she replied, smiling sleepily back at me. "What are your plans for the day?"

"Well, unfortunately, I have to work at noon."

"Oh. What time is it anyway?" At her question, I glanced at my phone.

"It's about 9:30."

"Well, how about I make us some breakfast? And then I'll probably do some yoga in the studio if you want to join me."

"That sounds lovely. Let's start with breakfast and then see what I have time for," I replied, warmed that she still wanted to spend time with me before we went about our days.

We both got out of bed, and I took a visit to the bathroom, doing my business and then swishing with some mouthwash I found before heading out to the kitchen. Anna was already pulling stuff out of the fridge for our meal, dancing to the music she had playing.

"How do breakfast burritos sound?" she asked, her back still to me.

"Delicious," I replied, coming up behind her to wrap my arms around her and pull her body against mine, kissing the side of her neck. "Not as delicious as you though," I added as I scraped my teeth along her skin.

She moaned and tilted her head to the side to give me better access. Encouraged, I let my hand wander down her stomach and slip under the waistband of her pants. I latched on to her ear with my teeth just as my fingers glazed her clit. She sucked in a sharp breath and pushed herself into the contact. I swirled my fingers against her, pulling her tighter against me. Within less than a minute, she was detonating. After she came down, I gently pulled back, giving her another soft kiss on her neck and a swat on the ass. She yelped out of surprise and turned toward me with laughter and pleasure written across her face.

"That's one way to start the morning," she said, laughing as she leaned over to give me a kiss on the lips, before turning back to cooking.

"Do you need help with anything?" I asked.

"You could pour some drinks for us if you want."

I nodded, suddenly realizing how thirsty I was. I opened her fridge to find my favorite apple juice sitting there. I poured us each a glass and downed half of mine before I even gave Anna hers. She did the same thing as I grabbed the teakettle that was on her stove and filled it with hot water. It was adorable, white with black polka dots, and the whistle said "Whistle while you Work." I smiled at it, thinking it was something that I would've bought for myself.

"All my tea is in that cupboard over there."

I opened it to find more tea than I'd ever seen in someone's home. I laughed, slightly overwhelmed. She turned and smiled at me.

"I like tea." It was perhaps the biggest understatement ever. "The ones on the left are caffeine free. The lavender honey and the mint are my favorites. The mint has caffeine and the other doesn't." I appreciated her narrowing it down for me.

I took the mint tea off the shelf and got out two bags. The water was boiling, and by the time I was finished getting our drinks, Anna was turning off the burners, our breakfast ready.

She set our food down, hers with bacon, mine without. We dug in, both starving after the night before. It was delicious and I moaned my appreciation. I couldn't remember the last time someone made me breakfast, and I stared at her, smiling at how normal and comfortable it all felt. She caught me staring.

"What? Do I have food all over my face?" she said with a full mouth, making me chuckle.

"No, siúcra. You look beautiful," I said sincerely, making her blush.

"Well, I'm sure that orgasm you gave me helped a bit," she teased with a wink, this time making me blush. "I could return the favor before you leave instead of us doing yoga, if you want?"

I scooted my chair closer to hers and dragged my thumb across her lower lip, our breathing accelerating.

"Well, who could say no to that?" I whispered, licking my lips, her gaze following the movement.

"How about you return my clothes to me, and then hop that pretty little naked ass up on this table and I'll eat you for breakfast instead?"

I started stripping off her clothes before she'd even finished talking, and I could feel myself already getting wet from her words alone. She watched me closely, and by the time I was fully undressed, I thought the fire in her eyes would burn me alive.

I did as I was bid, and climbed up on the table in front of her, lying back and spreading my legs wide. I heard her take a deep, shuddering breath as her hands skimmed up the outsides of my legs. She met my gaze and gave me a roguish smile before burying her face between my thighs.

The last thought crossed my mind before I entered a blissful oblivion was that I would gladly start every single day like this with her.

Chapter 7

Anna

"I'll call you," Molly said, leaning in for another kiss before opening the front door.

"As long as you aren't speaking guy language, because they never call when they say they're going to," I teased.

"I definitely do not speak guy language. I wouldn't even know how to go about that."

I smiled and gave her one more kiss before shutting the door behind her. I leaned against the door, taking a deep breath before squealing in excitement. Well, I knew I was a lesbian. I had never felt like that with a man before.

Maybe a big reason why was because of my past. Suddenly, my dream from the night before flooded my mind, and the smile vanished from my face. It was pretty hazy. I definitely did not remember it all that well, but I could distinctly see my father and hear him yelling at me.

In the dream, he had found out that I had been with a woman. All I could remember from his yelling was him saying that it was "sinful," and that I was going to hell. My blood ran cold as I recalled that my stepbrother was in the dream too. I shuddered as I stepped away from the door.

I went straight to the bathroom and turned on the shower, needing to warm up after my recollection. I lathered my hair, wanting to get all the hairspray out from my date last night. My thoughts drifted back to Molly. I already liked her so much, but a big part of me worried about dragging her into all my baggage. I had a lot of it, and being with a woman was definitely a complication. I had a lot of mental walls up, and wasn't sure I could ever let anyone see inside.

I got out of the shower, and heard my phone chime with a text as I was toweling off. I wrapped the towel around my head and strode naked over to check it.

How did it go last night?

It was from Lauren. Just as I was about to reply, another one came through from Savannah, making me realize that it was our group text that we had named "Best Bitches."

Yeah, did you get laid?!

Not that it's any of your business, I replied, *but yes I did. And it was FANTASTIC.*

Yeah, baby! replied Lauren.

Can we come over tonight to hear all about it? asked Savannah.

Only if you bring me food. I already have wine here.

Any requests?

Oh please, you bitches know that I'll eat anything. But make sure there's dessert too.

I'll bring brownies, said Savannah.

I guess I'm on taco duty then. It's fitting for the upcoming conversation. That one from Lauren.

All I sent in reply was a gif of Minnie Driver flipping everyone off.

The girls showed up that night, laden with armfuls of food. As usual, we dug into the food and wine before we started talking. Once we already had a glass of wine each and were eating the brownies with forks straight from the pan, they started in. I was honestly surprised they lasted as long as they did.

"So, give us all the details. We've waited long enough," said Savannah.

"Yeah, I wanted to text you last night, but I didn't think that would go over very well," Lauren added.

"Well, I definitely know that I'm a lesbian now," I said, smiling and blushing slightly in a very un-Anna-like way as Savannah squealed and clapped her hands together.

"So, you said you guys did it?"

"Well, we did stuff. We didn't technically go all the way though."

"What does that mean for lesbians? Like with a strap-on or what?"

"I mean, I think everyone's definition is different, but that would be one of them. In my mind it's scissoring," I replied, my blush deepening. I was so used to talking about sex, but it was so different with a woman, especially it being my first time with one.

"Yeah, I would agree with that," Lauren said.

"What happened after?" Savannah asked.

"She spent the night, and then we had breakfast," I answered. "And then I might've had a second…meal."

"Oh my God! Did you eat her out on the table we are currently eating on?!" Lauren yelled at me.

"Maybe…" I replied, laughing my ass off at both of their expressions. "Oh, get those looks off your faces. I cleaned the fucking table."

"Are you guys seeing each other again?"

"She said she would call me. Plus things just felt so natural between us. Like I felt like I had known her for years." I didn't mention my nightmare, or the things I had told Molly about my mother. Neither of them knew, and I wanted to keep it that way. The less people knew about my past, the better, and the safer they would all be.

"Does that mean the same thing as when a guy says it?"

"No. I already asked her that," I said, but I hadn't heard from her all day, and was starting to doubt myself just a touch.

As if on cue, my phone chimed with a text. I glanced down to see Molly's name flash across the screen. I let out a relieved sigh as I opened up the message.

Still thinking about how sweet you tasted. Miss you already, siúcra.

You're making me wet. I miss you too. I texted back.

"Oh my God, you dirty little slut!" Lauren yelled, reading over my shoulder. I had clearly rubbed off on her when we were living together, because she never used to say shit like that.

"Well, stop reading if it offends you so much!" I yelled right back.

"At least we know she's definitely interested in you," Savannah said with a grin, having also read the texts.

When can I see you again?

I was going to go to a paddleboard yoga class in a few days. Want to come? You can stare at my ass the whole class again if you want ;)

Hey! How did you know I was staring at your ass?

I didn't, but I do now. I sent her the link for the class in three days.

Perfect. See you and your sweet ass then.

The girls and I continued chatting throughout the night, catching up on everything since we hadn't seen much of each other lately.

"Savannah, have you heard anything about Greg?" Lauren asked, not having been there the other day when she and I discussed it.

"Not since he got released. I make sure to carry my gun with me everywhere I go though," she replied. I could tell that she was anxious about it, but that carrying her gun made her feel more safe and in control. I nodded at her; I completely understood that.

"Speaking of which," Lauren said, looking at me, "you said you'd never been around guns before, but you handled them like a pro." She looked at me with skepticism all over her face.

I avoided her eyes as I pretended to pick some invisible lint off of my pants, my heart rate picking up. "Well, maybe I'm just a natural."

"I think you're full of shit," came Savannah's reply. I could hear the heat in her words. It wasn't the teasing we normally gave each other.

I glanced up at my two best friends and saw the hurt on both of their faces. I knew I was being a shitty friend by not confiding in them about my past, but I didn't know how to go about it, or if it was the best idea.

"Yes, I've handled guns before. I've had my concealed carry since I was twenty-one, and I carried a weapon with me illegally before that," I said quietly.

I heard Lauren's intake of breath, but they both smiled at me, not prying for further information. I exhaled a relieved sigh, grateful that they weren't pushing. Maybe this was how I should do things with them. Just give them little bits of information at a time when I was ready.

"We know that you have secrets, Anna. That's okay. You don't have to tell us everything, but don't lie to us. And if you need to talk about any of it, we're here," Savannah said, giving me a knowing look. She had hid her fair share of baggage when we all first started hanging out. If anyone would understand, it would be her. I reached out and grasped her hand, giving it a tight squeeze in gratitude before letting go.

"Do you bitches want to go to the shooting range with me again soon?" I asked, knowing they probably hadn't gone in a while, and they needed to keep up their practice if they were going to be carrying those around.

"Yes! Let's go next weekend," Lauren exclaimed. I knew she was really enjoying shooting, especially after it had saved her husband's life. We firmed up the plans as we had one more glass of wine. They left soon after, and I was left to my thoughts, darker ones, as I thought about the reason I had to carry a gun with me since I was sixteen…

Chapter 8

Molly

I got to the lake at 11:40. I had never done paddleboard yoga before, but I was really looking forward to it. I loved the water. Probably because I grew up around it in Ireland. We lived right along the shoreline when I was younger, and being here in Colorado, while I loved it, made me miss the water.

I walked up to the instructor, and from the looks of it, I was the first one there. We chatted pleasantly while we waited for the others to show up.

"So, have you done one of these classes before?" Christine, the instructor, asked me.

"No. I actually have never been paddleboarding before, but I'm really excited about it."

"Are you nervous?"

"A little bit," I admitted.

"Well, don't worry, I always go over all the safety stuff and how to actually use the board before we go out there, and it's not too hard, especially since we're on a lake instead of an ocean. That's when it gets trickier with all the waves and currents."

I nodded and smiled at her just as Anna came up behind me, swatting my ass. I yelped, not expecting the contact, especially in public.

"Hey, gorgeous," she purred in my ear.

"Well, hey yourself," I purred right back. We held each other's gaze. When it became heated and we started inching toward one another, the instructor cleared her throat. We glanced at her, me smiling somewhat sheepishly, and Anna grinning like a cat who caught the canary. Christine just gave us a knowing smirk before greeting whoever else was arriving.

Within fifteen minutes, the rest of the class had shown up and she had gone through the safety tutorial. I took a deep breath to calm my nerves, and then got onto the board. They pushed me off and I paddled away, starting on my knees.

"Lookin' great, baby!" Anna shouted to me as she took off just behind me.

After a minute or so on my knees, I finally felt comfortable enough to stand. It took me a second to adjust, and there was a split second where I thought I was going to fall into the water, but I stayed on, smiling to myself. Anna was next to me a second later, and as I looked at her, with the water and the mountains around us, I knew that this was going to be one of those moments that I remembered forever. She turned to me, giving me a bright full smile, and I knew she felt the same way. I could feel it.

A few minutes later, we got to the middle of the lake where the instructor told us we were all meeting, and soon after we were all anchoring our boards. I closed my eyes for the start of class and we all took some deep breaths. I did yoga often, but this was a completely new experience for me, and I loved every second of it. The water was softly swaying my board and my body back and forth, there was a wonderful cool breeze on my face, which felt nice with the sun beaming down on my body, and a bird was singing in the background. It was literally perfect. There was no other way to describe it.

We started to move, and all the motions were so much harder. Every time I changed positions, I had to concentrate on not falling into the water. I was sure it was going to happen at some point, but I would do all I could to delay it, and I definitely did not want to be the first one in the water. Ten minutes later, the first splash happened. As the middle-aged woman came up, we all clapped and smiled at her. After that, it was like she opened a floodgate, because three more people fell in. We clapped with every new person, and I was feeling pretty good that I had yet to succumb.

Halfway through class, Christine announced we were going to do paired poses. Anna paddled over to my board and climbed right on next to me. Since we were on such a small surface, we had to get close to each other, which was fine by me. The first pose had Anna behind me in down dog. I got into the same position in front of her but then lifted my feet to put on her low back. Once I was there, I then lifted one of my legs into the air. I heard the instructor taking photos left and right, and I was excited to see how they all turned out.

The next pose was quite a bit harder. It started with Anna lying on her back one way, and me lying facedown on top of her the opposite way, my feet by her face and vice versa. Before we moved, I discreetly reached underneath me, and brushed my fingers along her pussy, just to tease her. I heard her sharp intake of breath before I felt a hard slap on my ass.

"Oops, my hand slipped," she said with amusement and lust coating her voice. I chuckled before we got back to it.

The next step was putting our hands on each other's ankles. Then, Anna would sit straight up, her arms and my legs above her head, each of us in the shape of an L, both forming a box together. We got into position, barely, and just as I heard the camera, I tilted, and both of us tumbled into the water together.

We surfaced, laughing our asses off. I heard the clapping around us, and before we tried to get back onto the board, I pulled her against me, kissing her heatedly. We broke apart quickly and climbed back up. A couple people, including the middle-aged woman, gave us slightly judgmental looks, but the instructor smiled at us and launched back into the lesson. I didn't care that they were judging us; I wasn't going to let anything ruin this perfect day.

We finished up the class, and Christine told us that we could stay on the lake for another twenty minutes or so if we wanted to keep paddleboarding. We of course took off and went the opposite way of everyone else. We took our time paddling to the farthest side of the lake than where we started, and then turned around to head back to shore.

"Race you back," Anna said mischievously.

"What does the winner get?" I asked.

"How about the winner gets to plan out our entire next date? All of it will be a surprise for the other one."

"Perfect."

"Three, two, one—GO!" Anna took off before I realized what was happening. I quickly started paddling away after her, smiling as I dug my paddle harder into the water. While she had started off ahead of me, I was catching up to her. Just as I was about to pull in front of her, she turned right into my board so that I wouldn't beat her, but it did more than that. As my board ran up onto hers, my balance was thrown off and I fell into the water. As I emerged, Anna was laughing her ass off.

"Are you okay?" she got out between giggles.

Instead of replying, I swam up to her, grabbed her hand, and yanked her off her board. She screamed as she plunged into the water beside me, and it was my turn to laugh.

"You bitch!" she yelled as she surfaced, splashing me. After about a minute of us soaking each other and pulling the other underwater, Anna pulled me in close to her, our bodies flush, my chest rising and falling quickly from our playing and from her closeness. I could feel my nipples pebbling under my shirt as they brushed against her breasts. I swept the hair from her face as I leaned closer.

"I won," she breathed into my mouth before sealing our lips together, stealing the air from me.

I don't know how long we stayed there, treading water and rubbing against each other, but when I started shivering from the cold, we climbed back onto our boards and paddled back to shore.

When we returned, everyone had already left, and Christine was waiting for us, looking a little impatient.

"Sorry, Christine. We got a bit carried away," Anna said, looking a little guilty. We had forgotten that she was waiting for us, and probably exceeded our twenty minutes.

"Yeah, I could tell," she said. While her voice had an edge of frustration, her eyes twinkled and there was a slight smile on her lips.

"That was a great class," I said. "I've never done anything like that before. I loved it."

She smiled fully as she replied, "Good. You should both try my glow class next time. I put glow sticks on the bottom of the boards and we go out once it gets dark."

We assured her that we would before heading to our cars. I lingered, not quite ready to part from Anna, but not wanting to seem clingy. I noticed Anna was lingering too, and just when I decided to see if she wanted to do something else with me, she spoke.

"I don't want to go our separate ways yet. Do you have to be anywhere?"

I breathed a sigh of relief as I smiled at her. "No, I'm free. What did you have in mind?"

"I'm not sure. I just don't want to say goodbye to you yet."

"How would you feel about doing something with needles…?" Her only reply was a wicked smile.

Chapter 9

Anna

"So which do you want to do first? My acupuncture or your piercing?" I asked Molly as we got into my car. We decided to leave hers at the lake.

"Well, I have acupuncture needles at home. Do you have piercing stuff?"

"Not at my apartment. How about this, we can go to the shop first and do your piercing, and then we can go to your house after to do the acupuncture." Molly nodded and smiled at me and we took off. "Do you have any piercings?"

"Just my ears. I got them done when I was twelve at Claire's."

I had to contain my shudder. All piercers hated hearing those words. Claire's was the worst place to get a piercing. Or any place really that used a piercing gun. Those things were dirty and disgusting. So many people ended up getting infections from them. Not to mention the terrible instances when the gun would get jammed while it was piercing someone.

"Are you nervous?" I asked.

She huffed a laugh. "A little."

"It's okay. I'm a little nervous about the acupuncture too," I admitted.

"Why? I thought you loved needles."

"I do, but sometimes I get nervous about things I've never done before."

She nodded, as if she completely understood.

"Have you decided what you want me to pierce yet?" I purred, a seductive lilt to my voice. The thought of putting a needle in her turned me on.

"Well, I've always wanted my nipples pierced," she breathed. I whipped my head toward her in surprise at her words. "But I don't think I'm quite ready for that. So maybe my nose?"

"I would very much like to pierce your nipples someday, but I agree. Let's do a not-so-intense piercing first," I said, taking a deep breath and giving her a sultry smile. She blushed slightly at the words. That was something that I loved about her. She wasn't innocent by any means, but because of her complexion, I could always tell when I said something she liked.

She took my hand in hers as I drove us on. I turned up the music and sang along as we went. I felt contentment settle deep in my bones. I never thought I would be able to feel this way with all the shit I had been through. I sent up a quick "Happy, thank you, more please" to the universe, feeling very grateful this wonderful woman came into my life, and gave her hand a squeeze at the thought.

A couple minutes later, we were pulling up to the shop. I could feel Molly's hand starting to sweat slightly in mine, the only sign that she was feeling nervous.

"Oh, you'll get to meet Savannah too. She and Lauren are my best friends," I told her, excited by the prospect. Molly's eyes got slightly bigger and her hand started to sweat just a little more, and I realized that I just made her more nervous. "Don't worry, you guys will love each other. She's super fun and laid-back. Ready?"

She nodded, taking a deep breath before making her way out of the car.

I followed her and grabbed her hand again before she could get too far ahead of me. I wanted the shop to see and know what we were to each other so that my male coworkers wouldn't immediately start hitting on her. Like they did with everything with a vagina.

Savannah was at the front desk as soon as we walked in. She looked up when she heard the front door chime, and had her client face on until she saw me. She looked from me to Molly and then a huge smile spread across her face. I squeezed Molly's hand one more time before turning to Savannah.

"Hey, bitch," I said.

"Hey, yourself. What are you doing here today? It's your day off."

"I know, but milady wants a piercing, so here we are. Savannah, this is Molly." Molly let go of my hand so she could shake Savannah's, smiling politely at her.

"It's so nice to finally meet you! Anna has told me so much about you," Savannah said, wrapping her in a hug instead of grabbing her hand. Molly looked slightly surprised before smiling even bigger and returning the gesture. "So, now that we've met, I've been thinking we need to go on a triple date. Me and Charlie, Lauren and Nix, and you two. What do you guys think?"

"Let the woman breathe, bitch," I jumped in, not wanting Molly to be overwhelmed.

"No, it's okay. I would love to," Molly replied.

"Great. I'll get Lauren in on it and we can start planning."

Just then Jared, another tattoo artist, came up. He was the biggest flirt in the whole shop. Savannah and I exchanged a look.

"You lookin' for a tattoo, darlin'?"

"Oh, fuck off, Jared. She's my girlfriend, for fuck's sake," I said, putting my arm around Molly. Jared's eyebrows rose almost up into his hairline, but I barely noticed as Molly whipped her head toward me, blushing deeply again, a slight smile grazing her lips. I led her to my station before Jared or Savannah could say anything.

"Girlfriend, huh?" she asked.

"Well, I'd like you to be. Is that okay with you?" My heart pounded hard against my chest as I waited for her to answer.

"I guess," she teased, leaning in to brush her lips against mine in a soft, but claiming kiss. I smiled against her mouth. We broke apart as we heard one of the guys wolf whistle. I flipped them all off before turning to my station. I washed my hands and put some gloves on before wiping everything down. I took out the selection of jewelry I had and she chose a simple small black stud. I quickly cleaned it before setting it beside all my tools. I wiped her left nostril down with antiseptic and made a tiny mark on her nose where I planned to pierce her.

"Go check that in the mirror to see if you like it," I told her, slapping her ass as she got up to look. She came back smiling and nodding before sitting back down in front of me. I picked up my needle and receiving tube. I put the tube on the inside of her nose, checking it multiple times against the mark that I made. "Ready?" I asked her.

She took a deep breath, and said, "Hit me with your best shot, siúcra."

On her next exhale, I shoved the needle through her nose. Her eye immediately started watering, and in the next second, I pushed the piercing through the hole I made, making her wince slightly.

"All done." I handed her a tissue and she wiped at her watering eye. "See that wasn't so bad, huh?"

"No. Except you didn't warn me about my eye spilling water everywhere," she admonished. "But now, every time I look at my face, I will see your mark on me." She gave me a sultry smile, and I felt like I was about to combust. I leaned in, careful of her nose, to give her a searing kiss, biting her lip as I was at it. Her moan filled my mouth, and I broke away before things could get too intense. I looked around the shop to see all the guys I worked with collectively drooling all over themselves and staring at us like we were the juiciest pieces of meat they'd ever seen. I gave them all the double bird before grabbing Molly's hand and leading her back up front.

"Well, that was some display you ladies put on. I won't hear the end of it all day long, so thanks for that," Savannah teased as we reached the front desk.

"Fuck off, cunt," I retorted, giving her an air kiss and a wink, slapping ten dollars on the counter to pay for the jewelry.

"So, when do you guys want to shoot for our triple date?"

"Maybe a few weeks out?"

"Sounds great. I'll chat with Lauren and we'll come up with something."

"Okay, well, we're going to take off. This one wants her turn putting some needles into me," I said with another wink, Molly blushing and Savannah chuckling as she leaned in to give me a friendly kiss on the cheek, and we headed out.

When we were safely back in the car and headed toward Molly's place, I asked, "So, what did you think?"

"You were right. I loved her." I smiled at her words. Tension I didn't know that I was carrying melted away. I was relieved that they liked each other.

"I knew you would. Are you sure you don't mind going on that triple date? I can postpone it if you aren't feeling up to a big group thing yet."

"No, it sounds great. I've met Lauren before and liked her too, so it will just be their guys that I haven't met yet. It will be a fun group."

I reached over and grabbed her hand, squeezing it in thanks.

We pulled up to her house not long after. It looked fairly small, but that was understandable since she lived alone. From the looks of it, I had a theory that it was actually the servants' quarters for the much bigger house right next door. It was only one story, and pink, which was surprising.

"Before you say anything, I know it's pink. I haven't gotten around to painting it yet."

"Hey, I like it."

She rolled her eyes at me. "Yeah, sure you do."

She opened the front door, and the next second I was looking around her space. I felt like it was an insight into who she was, and it was so refreshing. Not that Molly was standoffish, just that she had a sense of privacy to her, and I didn't feel like I'd even scratched the surface of her yet.

It was kind of a mix between farmhouse and Native American. The main space was all open. She had hexagon shelves on her wall with all sorts of plants inside, which were right above a light brown cloth couch with Indigenous-style pillows and blankets. Another wall had paintings with all sorts of animals ranging from llamas to cows.

Her kitchen had herringbone tiles on the walls and open shelving. It wasn't large, but she made good use of the space, taking advantage of every available nook without making it look crowded. There were hanging lights over her counters and a retro-looking farmhouse fridge and sink, which also had a black-and-white-checkered rug in front of it.

She took me to her bedroom next. It was very simple. She had a dark wrought iron bed frame in front of a dusty pink wall, and the rest were painted a light gray. Her comforter was white and she had different black-and-white-patterned throw pillows and blankets. Above her bed were three pictures of the moon in its different phases.

"Well, what do you think?"

"It's very beautiful and homey. I must say too that you are much tidier than I am," I added with a smile.

"I don't like to have too many things, so it makes it easier. Do you want any water or anything before we start?"

"Yes, please. And can I use your bathroom?"

"Of course. Why don't you go and I'll grab your water while you're in there," she said, gesturing to the attached restroom.

It was also beautiful in this room. She hadn't left one area of her house undone. There were black hexagonal tiles on the floor, and white subway tiles in the shower. She had a mustard-yellow shower curtain and a rug that said "Rise and Shine" with a sun on it. I smiled to myself in her wood-framed mirror before doing my business. I came back out a minute later, sniffing my hands after using her lavender-scented soap, and finding her setting my water on her nightstand.

"Are you okay doing it on the bed?"

"Oh, I'm definitely comfortable doing it on your bed." I winked, coming up behind her to kiss her neck as she chuckled. "How do you want me?"

"On your back," she breathed into my mouth as she turned to kiss me. "Do you have any concerns or anything you want me to work on?"

I smiled as she slid into acupuncturist mode. "Well, I don't know. I'm not really sure what sort of things you can help with since I've never done this before."

"More things than you think, honestly. People are usually surprised by how much we can actually do. Anxiety and depression, headaches, muscle tension, fertility, bad periods, you name it."

"Well, I do get headaches and bad periods." I took a deep breath and divulged something that not a lot of people knew about me. "I also struggle with anxiety and depression," I said quietly, avoiding her gaze.

When I looked up, she was nodding and looking up as if into her head to figure out where she was going to stick the needles, not even fazed at the little tidbit I just shared with her. I let out a relieved exhale, glad that she wasn't making a big deal out of it or asking me more questions.

"Okay, great. Lie on the bed face-up for me."

"Do I need to take anything off?"

Her eyes locked on mine and heated. "Not unless you want to."

"What if I want to take off everything?" I asked, my voice dripping with sex.

A beautiful blush rose on her cheeks. "As much fun as that would be, maybe we should save it for another time when you're more used to acupuncture. Besides, I don't think I would be able to control myself if I had to work on you with your glorious body staring at me."

I chuckled, swiping my finger between her legs before doing as I was told and lying down for her. She shook her head at me, a smile on her face before grabbing a handful of little packages.

"Are those the needles?"

"Yes. Do you want to see them?"

I nodded and she opened one of the packages. The tiniest needle I'd ever seen came out. My eyebrows rose in surprise. I didn't realize they would be so small.

"I told you they weren't big. You barely feel them. Now just relax and I'll get started."

I took a deep breath, closing my eyes and trying to calm my anxiety. I felt her fingers on my arms first. It was as if she was trying to learn everything she could from my body.

Before I could anticipate it, I heard a sound like a small spring but hardly felt anything. I opened my eyes to see a needle sticking out of my arm, and in the next second Molly was placing the second needle. I watched as she decided where to put it and gave the top of the needle a sharp tap, making the spring sound again, taking what looked like a small tube away after.

On and on she went. When she finished with my arm, she moved onto my legs and feet. I felt these more than the ones in my arm. There was a tiny pinch, and with some of them, a sharp zing. Those made me gasp. It wasn't a type of pain I'd ever felt before.

She finished my arms and legs, put one on my sternum, all along where the back of my neck met my skull, which I thought would get in the way, but she was able squeeze them in in the gap between my neck and the pillow, the tops of my shoulders, my third eye, and the very top of my head. Finally, she looked at me and asked, "How do those all feel?"

"Okay, I think."

"There are some that I want to do on your ears. They're really good for anxiety, but they can be a bit painful. Would that be okay with you?"

I nodded, grimacing as the needles moved. *Note to self, don't move any muscles with needles in them.* She took five needles out and put them all on the outer part of my right ear. They were painful, but as soon as they settled, a pressure lifted from my chest. I couldn't believe the lightness that I felt from them automatically.

"Still okay?"

"More than okay." I smiled at her, a bit of emotion in my voice at the relief I felt.

She smiled knowingly at me. "I can tell that it's already helping you. Okay, I'm going to leave you alone for a while. I'll just be in the next room. Let me know if you need me and I'll check on you in a bit, okay? Want me to cover you with a blanket before I go?"

"Yes, please."

She gently laid her throw blanket over me, careful of the needles, before walking out and shutting the door gently behind her.

I took another deep breath and closed my eyes, settling into the bed and needles more. Before I knew it, I was in a deep sleep, only it didn't feel like I was asleep. I felt aware of everything around me, but I knew that when I eventually opened my eyes I would feel extremely well rested and like I just woke up from an amazing nap. I almost felt myself floating above my body and around the room. I heard the door open sometime later, but I had no clue how long it had been. I stayed exactly as I was, not ready to come out of the deep meditative state that I was in. The door shut a second later, and I continued floating.

Minutes, hours, or days later, I opened my eyes. I felt exactly how I thought I would, like I'd just had the best nap of my life.

"Molly," I called.

A second later, the door opened. Molly waltzed in, smiling.

"How do you feel?"

"Amazing," I said. I then described the sensation I had been feeling. She nodded along as I talked, like she knew exactly what I was talking about, taking the needles out as I spoke.

"That's incredible that you got that sensation on the first session. Usually people only experience that a couple times, and it's usually after they've had acupuncture before. I've only experienced that twice. It is an amazing feeling."

I sat up a moment later and chugged the water that was on the nightstand next to me. "How long was I out?" I asked.

"For about an hour. Just over."

"Is that a long time?"

"It is for a newbie. Usually acupuncture virgins don't fall asleep and they only last about a half hour."

I nodded, drinking more water. My brain felt a little fuzzy and I was grateful that I didn't have to leave right away. Molly climbed into bed with me a minute later and we lay next to each other, just breathing the other in. It was refreshing. I didn't have on my normal mask that I did with everybody else. I felt like I could really be myself with her.

"I can feel how grounded that made you, and I'm glad."

I looked at her, thinking I would feel a wave of anxiety at her words, but nothing came. Just deep comfort. "You've said things like that before. What do you mean?" I asked.

"I'm an empath, Anna. I can sense other people's emotions and energy. Not all the time, and it's much more pronounced as I start to get to know the person. I think I've always had it, but it became more heightened after I started doing acupuncture. I started tuning in to energy and how it moves through the body."

"So, when you say you feel it, how? Like what does it feel like for you?"

"Sometimes it's very subtle. Like I will just feel an emotion for no reason at all, but it's not front and center, just kind of in the back of my head. Other times, it will hit me like a freight train. Those are the hardest ones to deal with, and I have to remind myself and really focus my attention on the fact that it's not my emotions I'm feeling. Once I make that distinction, it's a little easier for me to push that feeling away and discover how I'm feeling."

"It sounds exhausting. I don't think I would like that."

"I definitely didn't like it when I first figured it out, but now that I've come to hone it and process it better, it's actually become kind of a gift. Especially with what I do. It can also make my job that much more rewarding. I can feel people's negativity when they show up, and then through my work, I can feel the transformation when they leave."

"I never would have thought of that. It's very cool."

She nodded, smiling at me. "I know you probably don't want to, but if you ever need someone to talk to about anything, I mean your feelings or anything, you can always talk to me. I'll never judge," she ranted a bit.

"Thank you. I might tell you someday, but not quite yet. I have a lot of baggage, and I don't want to scare you off quite yet," I joked, trying to lighten the mood.

"I don't think anything you could tell me would scare me off," she said, then quietly followed it up with, "I think I've been looking for you my whole life."

I gasped at her words, delight filling me up. I leaned over and kissed her softly. "I've been looking for you too," I whispered into her mouth.

She moaned before grabbing me and pulling me on top of her. I smiled against her lips as I realized that I was ready to go all the way with her.

Chapter 10

Molly

Anna's words undid me. I had never felt like this with anyone before, and knowing that she felt the same way was earth-shattering. It snapped something inside of me, and as soon as I pulled her against me, I could feel that she was having the same reaction I was. I knew right then that she was the woman I was meant to spend my life with.

I attacked her mouth more fiercely, and she responded in kind, biting my lip in her urgency. I moaned loudly, wrapping my legs around her waist, getting as close as I possibly could. I broke away to trail my lips down her neck as I reached down to tug her shirt over her head, reveling in the fact that she wasn't wearing a bra. I grazed my fingertips over her nipple piercings, flicking them repeatedly. She ground herself against me as I sucked hard on her neck. I was claiming her, leaving my mark on her skin so the world could see that she belonged to me.

"Fuck yes. Mark me, Molly. Leave me a necklace of hickeys. I'm yours," she groaned, gripping my hair and shoving me farther into her neck, of course being mindful of my new piercing.

I groaned against her skin, her words making me impossibly wet as I did what she asked, biting her every now and then.

She leaned back, taking me with her so she could start stripping off my clothes. When we were both fully naked, she attacked my lips again. Her hands began roaming my chest, teasing my already sensitive nipples, pulling and tweaking them so they became hard as pebbles. My hands automatically went to her ass, gripping it and kneading her tight cheeks with both hands as I pulled her more firmly to me. I spanked her hard before moving my fingertips to her pussy. She was completely soaked, allowing me to easily slip a digit inside of her. It was shallow because of the angle, but she didn't seem to mind as she pressed herself into my hand.

"Fuck me, Molly," she begged, breaking away to look down at me with so much heat in her gaze I thought she would set the bedroom on fire. She lay down next to me, spreading her dripping cunt for me. I leaned down, starting to fuck her with my mouth and fingers. She let me for just a moment before grabbing my hair and pulling me up to her mouth. "No, fuck my pussy with yours. I want to feel all of you." I groaned at her words.

"You want me, siúcra?"

"Yes, more than I've ever wanted anything. Please, Molly. I need you," she begged.

"Me too, Anna, me too," I whispered into her mouth. Pulling back, I shifted one of her legs to make way for my hips. I straddled her pelvis at an angle, looking into her eyes at the first touch of our bodies. I closed my eyes, reveling in the exquisite contact. I started moving, dragging our lips and clits together, and we both cried out at the sensation. I could feel our wetness mingling and spreading over us, giving a smooth glide to our motions. "Fuck, you feel so good."

A whimper was her only reply, her hands gripping the sheets next to her. I started picking up speed, already feeling myself closing in on my orgasm. Her hands reached around to guide me even faster. There was something very erotic, I thought, about the fact that we were basically masturbating with each other's bodies, moving the other in a way that felt best.

Soon our movements became frenzied, and we were grinding against each other so hard that my bed frame was slamming against the wall, but I couldn't bring myself to care. "I'm close," I told her, wanting her to go over the edge with me.

"Me too," she replied breathlessly, reaching up to pinch my nipples between her fingertips in an unforgiving grasp. I crashed over the edge, wailing my pleasure. Anna followed me, and as she did, I felt a huge surge of wetness between us, like a fountain shooting into me. It was a sensation I had never felt before, and it prolonged my pleasure until I thought I would never resurface.

When I finally came back to earth, I opened my eyes, meeting Anna's gaze. She was blushing furiously, looking slightly embarrassed.

"What's wrong?" I asked.

She didn't answer me, just glanced down to where our bodies still met. I followed her gaze and saw a huge wet spot underneath us. At first I was a little confused, until she said, "You made me squirt. I'm sorry it left such a huge mess."

All of a sudden, I remembered the wet sensation when we both came and it made so much sense. I had heard of squirting before, but I always thought it was a myth. The fact that I made her do that turned me on all over again.

"Say something, please," she said in a small voice, making me realize that I still hadn't responded to her.

"Siúcra, you just made me that much more attracted to you. That was probably the sexiest thing I've ever felt. I thought squirting was just an urban legend."

Relief and heat flooded her face as she smiled at me. "It is definitely not. I bet I could get you to do it too. It doesn't usually happen for me with just clitoral stimulation though. It took me by surprise as much as you. Well, maybe not quite as much. Sorry, I should've warned you first." She smirked at me in a very Anna-like way.

"Oh please, it was a pleasant surprise," I said as I ground against her again, the sensation different because of what had happened. She whimpered at the renewed motion. I knew we had both already come, but I couldn't stop myself from moving. "I can't stop, Anna. You feel so good," I admitted.

"Don't stop," she begged. "I'm not done squirting."

I moaned at her words and redoubled my efforts, excited to feel it happen against me again. Within moments she was wailing and spraying everywhere. I kept going and so did she, and when she finally seemed to be all out, I flipped us so that she was on top, wanting to feel her in control. We also switched up the position. My legs pulled back against my chest, her squatting over me, leaning against my spread legs. Within minutes she had me detonating again.

We lay next to each other, catching our breath. She looked at me, still breathing hard, before looking down at the bed. She was laughing her ass off seconds later. My gaze followed hers and I saw the bed was completely soaked. Then I noticed that I was also lying in what felt like a puddle, and I joined in laughing with her.

"I am so sorry," she said between fits of giggles.

"Stop apologizing. I liked it," I replied, smiling at her. "Want to take a shower with me?" She nodded and I got out of bed to turn the water on before heading back into the room and stripping the bed. Luckily I had an extra set of clean sheets. Anna was in the shower and steam was filling the bathroom by the time I came back in. I snuck in behind her, wrapping my arms around her waist and kissing the side of her neck as the water pounded on us. She moaned in my arms before turning around to face me.

"I've never felt this before. This all-consuming desire. I already want you again," she said, her arms around my neck and body pressed against mine as she looked into my eyes.

"I never have either. Guess that means we're made for each other."

"Yep. You're stuck with me, whether you like it or not." She smiled before pressing her lips to mine. I kissed her thoroughly before pulling back to grab the shampoo. She held out her hand and I squirted a big dollop in her palm before doing the same to mine. We lathered our own hair, taking turns to rinse off before doing the same with the conditioner. When it came time for the body wash, instead of giving her any, I washed her myself, enjoying the feel of her wet body under my palms, and her moans as I teased her with my fingers. She returned the favor, and the shower might have ended with us each giving each other one more orgasm before getting out.

By the time we were both dried and dressed (Anna in some of my clothes), it was already six thirty.

"Shit, we should probably go get your car from the lake," I said, remembering that we had left it there. It probably would've been easier if we had just driven separately, but I just wanted to be with her longer.

"Oh, that's right." We quickly retrieved it, and by the time we got back my stomach growled in protest of all the activities we had done in the afternoon without eating.

"Are you hungry? I could make us dinner and we could open a bottle of wine."

"That sounds amazing. I'm starving." Her stomach chose that moment to make an equally angry noise and we both laughed, making our way to the kitchen.

"What about mushroom fettuccine alfredo?" I asked. It was pretty much the only meal option since I was due to go grocery shopping soon.

"Yum. I love mushrooms. And I am not a great cook, so I will pour the wine."

We worked in companionable silence for a few minutes before she handed me my drink and then turned on some music on her phone. Within minutes she was shaking her hips all over my kitchen. I smiled to myself as I cooked.

"Oh my God. Is it almost done? It smells delicious, and you're making me drool," she complained.

"Seriously?" I laughed. "It's only been like five minutes. Why don't you sit down and drink your wine." She grumbled, but obeyed. "If you're that hungry, I have some French bread in my pantry, and some oil and vinegar to dip it in."

She jumped up excitedly to get it and before I knew it, she was swirling the bread in the oil and vinegar, moaning as she popped it into her mouth. She dipped another piece and held it in front of my mouth for me. I wrapped my lips around her fingers, giving them an extra swipe with my tongue before pulling back and chewing the bread. I watched her eyes latch on to my lips as her pupils dilated.

"Want more?" she asked, her voice husky with desire. I nodded and we repeated the whole process again. As she pulled her hand away, some oil dripped onto my lip and started down my chin. I lifted a hand to wipe it away, but before I knew what was happening, she had grabbed my wrist and her tongue was licking the oil off. I then felt her suck my bottom lip into her mouth, thoroughly cleaning it off for me. She gave it a small nip before pulling back. I almost pulled her to me to finish what she started, but she danced out of my grasp, spanking me before sitting back down with her bread and wine.

"Feed me, wench."

I laughed, turning back to the food. It was done soon after and we sat at my breakfast bar with some candles lit, and Nat King Cole playing on my Bluetooth speaker. I waited for her to try my food, for some reason wanting her to really like my cooking. I wasn't disappointed.

"Okay, so I'm moving in so that you can cook every single meal for me. This is glorious." I knew she was kidding about the moving-in thing, I mean, of *course* she was, but as soon as she said it, I couldn't help but picture it. I wanted her here. In my space with me. Every day.

I must've had a strange look on my face, because in the next second she said, "What's wrong? Oh God, was it the moving-in comment? I didn't mean it. I take it back. Don't freak out," she rushed on.

"Siúcra, stop. I'm not freaking out. I just like the idea way too much," I said quietly, now feeling nervous she was going to be the one scared off.

Anna gave me a nervous smile. "Oh. I know it's too soon, but I like that idea too."

I blushed slightly, my skin giving away all my thoughts, and I grasped her hand tightly in mine, brushing my thumb over the back of hers. I leaned in to give her a soft but swift kiss on the lips before finally digging into my food.

We ate in companionable silence, Anna occasionally humming to the music even through a mouthful of food, making me smile. When we were both finished, I went to clean up both of our plates, but Anna batted my hands away and grabbed them before I could stop her.

"You cooked, I'll clean."

"Do you want anything sweet for dessert?" I asked.

"You." My blood heated at those words, and despite the fact that we had already fooled around multiple times that day, moisture flooded between my legs.

I grabbed our wine, giving her a glance before I sauntered to the bedroom. "Come to bed when you're done with the dishes," I ordered her. She gave me a sinful smile before returning to her task. I shut the door behind me, not wanting her to see what I was up to. I set our wine on the nightstand and opened the top drawer to reveal all my lingerie. I had an obsession with it. I quickly selected my favorite item, a dark emerald green silk baby doll, with a plunging V neckline, the borders trimmed with black lace. I quickly stripped and donned it before running to the bathroom to check my makeup. I fluffed my hair, giving it a just-fucked look, and applied a sinful red lipstick to my mouth. I also put on some massive black heels, which I called my stripper shoes. I gave myself a once-over. I looked thoroughly fuckable.

I walked back into the room, relieved that Anna wasn't done yet, and took a big gulp of wine before sprawling out on the bed. I had that awkward moment where I tried to find the sexiest position to be in before she came into the room. I just got comfortable when she opened the door.

She stopped, her eyes roaming over every inch of me. I watched as she swallowed loudly, her grip on the handle unforgiving.

"Dessert, indeed" was all she said before she launched herself at me.

Chapter 11

Anna

I woke the next morning in Molly's bed, spooning her from behind. I was surprised to realize that I hadn't had any nightmares, or woken up at all during the night. For a couple minutes, I just lay there, enjoying the feel of our bodies pressed together. I took a deep breath, the smell of Molly's shampoo filling my nose, and I let out a contented sigh.

Molly squirmed, slowly waking up. I pulled her tighter against me and nuzzled her neck. She moaned softly before turning to face me.

"Good morning, siúcra."

"Good morning yourself," I replied.

"How did you sleep?"

"Like I had a day full of orgasms from a beautiful woman, who then fed me a delicious dinner."

A blush rose onto her cheeks as she smiled brightly at me. "Good. Me too. Do you have to work today?"

"Yes," I answered, "I have to be there by ten." I glanced at the clock on her nightstand to see that it was already nine. "Shit. I don't think I'll have enough time to go home to get ready."

"You can get ready here. And we're pretty much the same size, so you can borrow some of my clothes if you need. I have lots of makeup too."

"Wow. It's so wonderful dating a woman. This would never be the case if you were a man. At least I would hope not," I joked, winking at her. "Mind if I take another shower? I think I smell like sex."

"I bet all the guys at the shop would love it if you didn't shower, but yes you can. I would join you, but if I did that, then I know I would make you late."

"I don't mind if you make me late," I said, suddenly not caring if I showed up for work at all.

She reached over me to smack my ass. "Go make that money, woman, so you can buy me lots of pretty things," she teased, getting up and scooting out of reach before I could change her mind.

"Ughhhh, fine," I complained, making my way to the bathroom. I left the door open as I turned on the shower and started stripping. I glanced at myself in the mirror and found three hickeys on my neck. One on each side, and one in the middle. Oh man, the guys were going to have a *field day*. I dragged my fingers across them, smiling. Well, she had certainly done as I asked and marked me. I loved it.

Steam started filling the room, the mirror fogging up, drawing my attention back to the shower. I put my hair up before stepping in. I quickly washed up, using Molly's body wash. I liked that I was going to be smelling like her all day, and I knew that every whiff would bring a smile to my face.

When I stepped out, Molly was nowhere to be found, but I heard sounds coming from the kitchen. She must have heard the water turn off, because in the next minute she shouted at me to use and take whatever I needed.

I started with clothes, selecting a pair of pretty lace cheeky plum-colored panties. She had a matching bralette, but my boobs were much bigger than hers, so I decided to forgo a bra altogether. I put on a tight tank top to keep my tits in place for the day, before finding a loose-fitting light gray shirt that had a rainbow on it with the words "Good Vibes" underneath. Finally, I grabbed some dark blue jean shorts with some rips in them.

I went back to the bathroom, finding her makeup case on the sink. I kept it simple, since I didn't have a lot of time. I put on blush, eyebrow pencil, a nude-colored eyeshadow, and mascara. I fluffed my sex hair in the mirror, figuring that was as good as it was going to get, and made my way to Molly in the kitchen.

She had a cup of tea sitting for me on the breakfast bar, and she was just finishing up our breakfast of scrambled eggs, avocado, and toast before turning to look at me. She dragged her eyes up and down my form, her eyes heating.

"Damn, if I don't like you in my clothes," she breathed, a blush rising on her cheeks.

I smirked at her. "I will wear your clothes every single day if it brings that look to your face." I leaned in to kiss her, intending it to be a quick peck, but her arm came around my waist and pulled me tight to her, deepening it. I moaned into her mouth, dragging my tongue along her bottom lip before hers came out to meet mine. Before I knew what was happening, she had her leg in between my own, and I was grinding against her. Her hands gripped my ass, urging me on.

"That's it, Anna," she breathed into my mouth. I moaned louder, her whispered words turning me on even more. I pushed her back against the counter and rubbed myself along her even harder. Within moments, I was detonating, liquid heat pooling into the panties I borrowed. I slowed my movements, and when I opened my eyes, Molly was watching me closely, her cheeks a furious red. She captured my lip between her teeth before breaking away. "That may have been the sexiest thing I've ever seen," she said, her voice rough. "Now eat your breakfast before it gets cold and you're late for work."

"Yes, ma'am." I quickly sat, light-headed from the quick orgasm. Suddenly ravenous, I inhaled my breakfast. Within minutes, my plate was cleared. I sat back, sighing, grabbed my tea, and took a nice, long drink. I looked over at Molly to find an amused but pleased look on her face. Her plate was still mostly full. "What?" I asked. "You worked up my appetite."

"Hey, I wasn't the only one involved. May I remind you that you started things just as much as I did, if not more so," she argued. Well, I couldn't deny that.

"I can't help it. You're just so sexy."

Another blush rose onto her cheeks as she smiled at me, taking another sip of her tea. "Right back at ya, baby."

I glanced at the clock to see that it was 9:45.

"Shit. babe, I have to leave, otherwise I'm going to be late." I quickly stood, getting my stuff together.

"I know, that's okay. I'll see you soon."

"Damn straight you will. I get to cash in on my surprise date for you." She smiled at that. I leaned down, giving her a brief but heated kiss. When I pulled back she looked contentedly dazed. "See you soon, lass," I said in a fake, albeit terrible Irish accent. I heard her laughter long after I walked out the door.

I walked into the shop to find Savannah wearing a shit-eating grin. I rolled my eyes at her as I passed, but was unable to stop myself from smiling. She followed me. Of course she followed me. It was Savannah after all.

"So, you two put on quite the show yesterday. Speaking of which, those are not your clothes."

"How would you know?" I asked, whirling toward her, eyebrows raised. Her eyes shot straight to my neck.

"Oh, you dirty little *slut*," she said, her grin growing wider.

"Fuck me. I've definitely worn off on you." I shook my head in exasperation. Now I knew what it was like to deal with my intense ass.

"Did you guys do the thing?"

"What thing?" I asked innocently, knowing perfectly well what she was referring to.

"Oh, bitch, just tell me!"

A sly smile crawled onto my lips, and I finally lived up to my reputation, screaming, "Yes, we did it!"

"I knew it. Give me all the dirty details."

"Oh, yes please," Jared said, having snuck in with Johnny, both of them having clearly heard what we were talking about. I rolled my eyes at them, but before I could tell them to fuck off, their gazes shot to my neck and the hickeys that were clearly on display.

"I think I've died and gone to heaven," Johnny said under his breath. He had been the one to wolf whistle the day before when Molly and I kissed. As much as I liked having Molly's mark on me, I wasn't looking forward to the attention I was bound to get from both of them all day.

"So how did the scissoring go?" Jared asked, making the gesture with his hands. I punched him in the arm hard, and pinched Johnny's underarm with my other hand.

"Too good for either of you to ever find out about. Now go fuck off." They reluctantly went to their stations, each being babies and rubbing their arms where I gleefully inflicted some damage.

"That was wonderful to watch," Savannah commented, a delighted smile on her lips, "but you know that it's only going to get worse with them, right? Especially if you bring her in more."

"I know. It's totally worth it. And maybe it'll stop Jared from hitting on me."

"Ha. That's never going to happen, but good luck with that. So, seriously. Give me the dirty details." She whispered that last part.

I proceeded to tell her everything. By the time that I was finished, she was fanning herself, looking somewhat turned on, surprisingly.

"What?" she asked. "Just because I'm not a lesbian doesn't mean that I don't get turned by the hotness of it." I laughed. Before we could continue the conversation, a client walked in.

"Hello, how can I help you today?" I asked, easily slipping into my professional persona, despite what we'd just been talking about. It was a twentyish-year-old girl who was blonde and looked like she just moved from Cali, which was a definite possibility. We had a lot of Californians moving to Colorado.

"I have an appointment with Jared for a tattoo of a butterfly," she said, attempting to look down her nose at me. It took all of my self-control not to roll my eyes.

"Come on back, sweetheart," Jared's voice came from around the corner. A flirty smile appeared on her face, her eyelashes already fluttering. As soon as she was out of sight I really did roll my eyes. Only Jared. I wonder where he had found this one. I bet she would be sticking around the shop much longer than she needed to after her tattoo was finished.

I turned to find Savannah behind me. She looked equally annoyed and disgusted.

"So anyway, I need to plan a date for me and Molly. I want it to be fun and unique. She knows it's happening, but she won't know what we're doing. Any ideas for me?" I asked.

"Well, it's summer so you could definitely plan an outdoor activity. Water World?" she asked, referring to the water park on the north side of Denver.

"I do love that idea, but our last date was water related. Let's mix it up a little bit. Ooh, one of those group biking bar things? You know, the ones where everyone is on the bike but it's really a bar and you all have to pedal?"

"You need a group to book one of those. Like ten people I think."

"Damn it," I said. I wanted this date to be fun and special and original.

"You know what? We're forgetting that you're dating a woman. A lot of the things that guys wouldn't be interested in doing she will probably love," Savannah said, making a good point.

"Like what?"

"Well, shopping for one. Or pedicures. Art walks. That sort of thing." I nodded along, exploring my new options.

"You know what we haven't done in a long time is go thrifting." The girls and I used to go to the thrift store all the time and we always had so much fun.

"Oh, bitch. I just had the best idea. What if you took her to the thrift store and you both chose outfits for the other one to wear on your next date?"

I smiled widely, imagining the ridiculousness that would come of that, and immediately loved the idea. "Do you think you could get Charlie to do that? It would be amazing if all of us dressed in ridiculous outfits for our triple date."

"Yes!" she exclaimed excitedly. "Shit, this is going to be so fun. I'll get Lauren and Nix on it too. Nix will absolutely hate it, I'm sure, but between Charlie and Lauren, they can get him to do it. It would also be awesome if we went to a fancy restaurant where we were bound to get some weird looks from people."

I laughed loudly, just picturing it. "Oh, this is going to be the most absurd thing we've ever done. The public will never know what hit them."

Chapter 12

Molly

A week later, I was at work. It was a slow day so I was at my desk in between clients. I hadn't seen Anna since she spent the night at my house. We had been texting every day, but between our opposite work schedules, we hadn't been able to get together. I was eating some yogurt, and looking over the schedule for the rest of my day, when she texted me.

What are you doing tonight? I smiled, hoping that we would finally be able to get together.

Nothing, why?

I'm cashing in the surprise date that I won on the lake. I'll pick you up at six.

You did not win, I argued, even though I was excited that she had planned a whole fun date for us.

I did so, now meet me at my house at six, wench!

I laughed, shaking my head as I got back to work.

It occurred to me when I got home that I had no idea what we were doing on our date. With that being the case, I had no idea what to wear. I figured that Anna would have told me if I needed to wear something fancy, so I kept it casual, donning a flowy black skirt with a gray tank top. Underneath, I was a little fancier, however, wearing a lace olive green bra and panty set. I kept my hair down and did my makeup fairly simple.

I got to her house at 6:03 to find her already in her car, just waiting for me to get there. I guess she didn't want me knowing where we were going on our surprise date, and wanted to drive us. I hopped in and she was pulling me in for a heated kiss before I could even shut my door.

"Ready?" she asked, slightly breathless by the time we pulled apart.

"When I have no idea what we're doing? Sure," I teased.

"Smart ass. You'll love it."

I grabbed her hand after she pulled out onto the street, holding it between us. She looked over to give me a satisfied smile. Ten minutes later, we were pulling up to ARC.

"My surprise date is you taking me to the thrift store?" I asked, bewildered.

"Hey, now. This is just the first part of the date. Besides, you haven't heard *why* we're at the thrift store," she defended, while still looking slightly nervous that I wasn't going to have fun.

"Well, I do love the thrift store. So, why are we here then?"

"We are going to pick out outfits for each other to wear on our triple date. Savannah and Lauren are making their guys do it with them too," she explained, a mischievous smile on her face. Oh fuck. This was going to be interesting. And hilarious.

I laughed loudly. "All right, but fair warning, you might end up in the ugliest outfit in the world for our date."

"Challenge accepted, baby," she replied, winking at me and looking delighted.

We walked into the store, hand in hand. The smell immediately hit me, the same one that all thrift stores have, like dirty clothes, old people, armpits, and cheap detergent. I breathed it in, smiling. I had not been thrifting in a long time, and I loved it. I was so excited we were here. And equally excited to find something absolutely ridiculous for her to wear.

"Best of luck, madam," I said to her, taking off to the women's department with her right on my heels. We looked through shirts first, finding some hideous selections that we were each thinking about for the other, including a pink vest with tassels hanging from the bottom, and a leopard long-sleeve shirt with so many frills on it that it was difficult to see how to even get it on. We also found some super cute stuff that we put in our carts to take home with us. That was the fun thing about the thrift store, you really had to hunt for the good pieces, but were sufficiently entertained by the horrible articles.

Within a half hour, our cart was full and we made our way to the dressing room to try on all of our stuff, both wonderful and horrifying. It took us longer to try on the clothes than it did to find them. We were laughing our asses off at the ridiculousness that was occurring, and I couldn't remember the last time I had that much fun.

We each spent around $50 because we bought so much stuff, and the search for the perfect triple date outfits had concluded. For me, Anna had selected a dress that had the absolute worst shape to it. Most of it was a blinding shade of sunset orange (that clashed horribly with my hair) with the exception of the portion above the sweetheart neckline that was tan, and it fell to about the knees. The orange section was made completely out of tulle, flaring out from the bust and puffing out at the bottom, getting bigger the farther down it went.

The dress I picked for Anna was the shiniest fabric I had ever seen in my life. I had no idea what it was made of, but it was metallic and felt super scratchy, almost like mermaid sequins, the type of material that gave me homecoming dress flashbacks. It was an iridescent pink to yellow (like strawberry lemonade), with flutter sleeves and a belted waist. The collar came up to her neck and the hem fell to about midthigh. I think overall, I had definitely won the ugliest outfit challenge.

"So, what next?" I asked.

"We're going to my apartment."

"The date is ending with your apartment? That's not very creative."

She gave me a secretive, mischievous smile before saying, "Whatever you say, darlin'." My eyebrows rose; she must've had something unique in mind for her to smile like that.

"Should I be nervous?" I asked.

"With me? Always," she replied, and her wink had my panties melting.

We walked into her apartment, and I didn't see anything special. I glanced at her in question. Instead of answering me, she poured us two glasses of wine, and handed me mine before she grabbed my hand and dragged me upstairs to her loft. When we got to the top, I let out a disbelieving laugh before taking a large drink of wine. I had a feeling I would need it.

She had moved all of her yoga stuff, and on the floor lay an enormous drop cloth. In one corner, she had a chair set up with a canvas and a set of paints next to it. When I looked at her in question, I found her clothes were already off, laying in a pile next to the stairs. She was leaning against the railing, watching my reaction and sipping her wine with a secret smile on her face.

"What are we doing?" I asked, breathless just from looking at her.

"We're going to paint each other. Naked."

"You mean like 'Paint me like one of your French girls, Jack'?"

She smiled at my reference. "Yes. Although I can't paint worth shit, so it will probably end up looking awful."

"I can't paint either," I admitted, laughing. This was going to be hilarious.

Sexy? Check.

Fun? Check.

Ridiculous? Check.

I had to hand it to her, her date hit all the right boxes.

"Well, why don't you get into position for me, siúcra?"

"I will once you take your clothes off too." I set my wine down, and held her eyes as I slowly stripped off my clothes. They landed right next to hers. She looked like she was going to reach for me then, but I scooted out of the way, grabbing my wine again before taking up the seat in front of the canvas. Very aware of the fact that I was naked, I sat up straight and gently crossed my ankles. I looked down at all of the supplies next to me. There were all the colors I could want, and multiple brushes. I, of course, didn't really know what I was doing, so I picked up a smaller-sized brush, and then went about pouring out some paint colors on the plastic plate laid out.

When I looked back at Anna, she was sitting on the drop cloth, facing me, her arms were behind her, supporting her weight, but what immediately drew my attention was that her legs were splayed open, knees bent, feet planted on the floor. Even from here, I could see the slickness already gathering between her lips. My mouth watered as I took my fill of her, and when my eyes finally met hers, they were blazing.

I took another drink of wine, steadying myself. I knew this wouldn't be an easy task, and that by the end of it, we were likely to tear the room apart in our frenzy to get to each other, but that's what made it so fun.

Ready, I swirled my brush in some paint and got started. Almost as soon as I started, I decided I wanted to go the black and white route, with maybe just a touch of red and pink. I finished the outline of her body, all in black, actually doing much better than I thought I would. I dragged a little bit of white through the black in certain areas to make it a little more dimensional. I then started on the finer details, using red for her mouth, and pink for the hearts that made up her nipples, and her slick swollen pussy. Every time I looked back at her, it seemed she became more and more drenched. By the time I finished it, my nipples were hard, I was panting, and I could feel my own slickness coating the insides of my thighs.

"Done," I breathed, my voice so rough I could barely get the word out. I took a drink to clear my throat and my head. I stood, moving my painting to make way for a fresh canvas for her. As I bent over to set it on the floor and rest it on the wall, I felt a single finger slide through my nether lips, and I gasped audibly, the sensation so intense it almost brought me to my knees. I stood quickly, whirling to face her, only to find her already seated in the chair five feet from me. I moved to touch her, and she only tsked at me.

"Not yet, lovely. It's your turn."

I growled my frustration, plopping down on the floor in front of her. I tried to figure out how to one-up her on the posing situation. Something to really drive her crazy, especially since she teased and then denied me. I ended up sideways to her, lying on my back, my knee closest to her slightly bent to hide my goods from view. I looked at her, my red hair fanning out around my head like a halo, while one hand made my way to my nipple, the other down to my pussy. I heard her sharp intake of breath before she narrowed her eyes.

"I know what you're doing," she stated, amusement and desire thick in her voice.

"What's that?" I breathed innocently.

She only shook her head, smiling, before she picked up the brush and got to work.

I slowly started stroking myself, my wetness coating my fingers. My other hand started plucking at my nipple, drawing it out and hardening it. A moan escaped my mouth, and Anna bit her lip, seeming to use all her concentration to keep painting. I kept my eyes on her the entire time, and ten minutes in she began shifting in her seat, occasionally pressing her thighs together. I smiled, enjoying watching her squirm as I pleasured myself. I began moving my fingers faster, my breath coming quicker, my moans louder. I knew a massive blush rose across my cheeks and chest, and I felt myself getting close. Before I could push myself over, a splash of something wet shot across my torso. I blinked down to find red, the color of my hair, splattered across me. Paint.

I looked at Anna incredulously. She smirked. "None of that. You don't get to come yet."

"Oh yeah? What are you going to do to stop me?" I asked, continuing my ministrations, still moving faster and bringing myself closer.

"Don't do it," she warned, challenge on every plane of her face. She wanted me to keep going. She wanted to do whatever it was she was going to do to make me stop.

I pinched my nipple, groaning loudly while I maintained eye contact with her. Her eyes flashed with delight as she stood and walked over to me. Before I could wonder what she was going to do, the tray of paints was tipped onto my body. I squealed in surprise, looking down at myself to find ten different colors covering my torso.

"Oh, you're going to get it," I said, crawling over to the table with the paints. I opened one and squirted it right at her chest. Before I knew what was happening, it was an all-out paint war. We were laughing and splashing each other over the drop cloth, and before long we were on the floor, rubbing our bodies together, trying to get as much of the paint onto the other person.

Within minutes, we were kissing and our bodies were rubbing together for an entirely different reason. We rolled all over that drop cloth, pinning each other. First with my face buried between her legs, finally getting to taste what my mouth watered for at the start of all this. She writhed beneath me, paint-soaked fingers gripping my hair and moving my head in time to the thrust of her hips against my face. I moaned as she screamed her climax, her orgasm coating my tongue.

Before she fully came down, I had her legs spread and my throbbing cunt rubbing against her own. I could feel the tremors against me and my own orgasm from before came closing in on me fast. I held out, wanting it to last a little longer, but it was difficult, especially when Anna's fingers clamped onto both of my nipples, applying an unforgiving pressure.

"Come for me. I want to feel you shudder against me," she breathed.

"Not yet," I replied, holding out with everything in me. I knew this orgasm was going to rip me apart and I wanted her right there with me. I wanted to feel her gush against me. "I want you to squirt for me again. Squirt all over me."

She whimpered at my words and moved more frantically against me. "Now," she said, pinching my breasts even tighter and spiraling me into my orgasm right as I felt her gush into me. Just as I knew it would, it destroyed me. It went on for what felt like forever, Anna continuing to spurt against me, soaking us both. When we were both completely spent, I collapsed on top of her. She stroked my back in gentle circles until our breathing calmed. I hummed against her neck, feeling completely content.

"Are you hungry?" she finally asked me, what could have been minutes or hours later.

"Starving."

"Want to order something?"

I nodded against her, feeling boneless, but I made myself get up. When I finally did, I laughed loudly. Anna was a huge mess; there was literally paint all over her, and the drop cloth was not only covered as well, but you could see our body shapes on it, and to me it was obvious as fuck what occurred.

"Well, that is going to be hung above my bed," Anna said with a smile on her face, gazing fondly at the drop cloth, as if she could see the whole scene playing out.

She grabbed her phone and we quickly ordered something on Grubhub before we carefully made our way to the shower. It was a good thing the food was going to take a while, because it took us forever to get clean. There was paint everywhere you could imagine. The worst was in our hair, and we had to wash it four times before most of it was out. There were still slight residues on us both, but at least we wouldn't be getting paint all over the apartment.

We dried off and both dressed in something comfy of Anna's. We grabbed our wine and plopped onto the couch with our Chinese food. Anna gave me the remote and I browsed through her list of movies on Vudu. I settled on *Seven Brides for Seven Brothers*. It seemed we each had a love for old movies.

"I grew up with this movie," she said suddenly. "It was one of my mom's favorites." I knew that she rarely talked about her past, so I was grateful for the tidbit she offered up.

"I love this movie too," I said, smiling and pulling her to me on the couch. "What was your mom like?" I asked gently.

She smiled sadly. "She was wonderful, radiant. Everyone who knew her instantly loved her. So vibrant and full of life, until the cancer. I think that the hardest part was watching her bright spirit dull and fade into nothing." I squeezed her, knowing that the only comfort I could offer was touch and a sympathetic ear.

"Well, I'm sure she would be very proud of the woman you've become." I looked down at her to see her expression shutter and harden.

"I'm not so sure about that," she replied quietly, subtly moving out of my arms. Before I could reply, she stood up, grabbed the empty food containers, and started cleaning up. "Come on, let's finish the movie in bed." I helped her clear the coffee table, and then hand in hand we went to bed.

Chapter 13

Anna

Molly and I were holding hands. That was the first thing I noticed. I glanced at her to find her smiling at me.

"Are you ready?" she asked. I furrowed my brow in confusion. I didn't know what she was referring to. Before I could ask her, we were walking through the door to a house. I glanced around in horror; it was my childhood home. I began frantically shaking my head. We couldn't be here. I went to turn around, ready to drag Molly with me, but found my stepbrother, Nathan, standing in front of the door. His arms were crossed, he was shaking his head at me, and he had a smug smile on his face.

"Oh no. You aren't going anywhere."

"Hannah? Is that you?" I heard my dad ask as he walked into the living room, my stepmother on his heels, looking at me like she always did, a disdainful smirk gracing her beautiful lips. "Have you finally come home?" His eyes were full of fatherly warmth, that was until he glanced down and saw my and Molly's fingers intertwined. "Who is this?" he asked, his voice full of reprimand and judgment.

I took a deep breath, no going back now. "This is my girlfriend, Molly."

"Girlfriend?" he asked, his eyes and voice becoming glacial. "You are no

daughter of mine." My stepmother behind him put a supportive hand on his arm, her eyes narrowed in disappointment.

"Where did we go wrong with you, Hannah?" she asked, tears forming in her eyes and breaking free as she shook her head, her big Georgia hair not moving an inch.

"Get out!" my father bellowed, pointing to the door behind us. Just before I went to comply, I felt a mouth at my ear.

"I'm coming for you, Hannah," Nathan whispered, his voice full of dark promise.

I woke up screaming. Molly's hand was on my back, stroking me in soothing circles. I took some deep breaths to calm my racing heart. I could still feel his hot breath on my neck, and I suppressed a shiver. I had tears gathering in my eyes that I really didn't want her to see. I pulled away from her momentarily, any touch setting me slightly on edge.

"Want to talk about it?" Molly asked understandingly.

I debated. I did want to tell her, but I didn't quite feel ready yet. I had kept my past hidden from literally everyone for over ten years. I wasn't ready to delve into it. And I think I would hate the sound of my real name on her lips. On anyone's lips, really. I took another deep breath, letting her touch calm me.

"No. Not yet, Molly. Someday, but not right now."

She nodded her head in understanding, holding her arms open for me to climb into. I did, snuggling my face against her chest. I let the sound of her steady breathing and even heartbeats lull me back to sleep.

The next morning, I woke early, still shaken from my dream. I left Molly sleeping in bed, and went to go make some tea. As I sipped, I thought about what, if anything, my dream meant. Obviously, the part with my dad and stepmom was self-explanatory. I always knew that my dad would never approve of me being with a woman. It was sinful. Plain and simple.

The part with Nathan bothered me though. I had a feeling it was more than just a dream. It felt more like a premonition. Something hot spilled into my lap, making me gasp. I looked down to find that I had spilled my tea; my hands were shaking uncontrollably. I made myself carefully set the tea on the table and take a few deep breaths to settle my racing heart. When I felt somewhat composed, I took my tea into the bathroom, deciding to take a hot shower. I'd always felt that there was nothing a hot shower couldn't cure.

When the water was as hot as I could stand, I made my way in. I laughed, looking down at myself. There was still paint on me. I almost didn't want to wash the rest off; it was such a lovely reminder of the fun we had the night before. The thought of what we had done and the heat from the shower was steadily chasing away my bad dream, turning my nervous tension into excitement. Just as I was thinking about reaching my hand down to touch myself, I felt warm, delicate hands wrap around my chest from behind.

"Good morning, beautiful," Molly uttered against my neck, her voice rough from sleep.

I reached around to grab her head, pulling her further into me, and pushing my breasts more firmly into her hands. "Good morning indeed."

She gently bit down where my neck and shoulder met, one of her hands moving lazily down my torso. I gasped as one of her fingers barely grazed my clit, and I moved my hips to grind against it. She merely chuckled and kept her barely there touch, slowly driving me insane. She was working me on all fronts, her other hand still teasing my breast, while her mouth licked up the side of my neck and sucked my earlobe between her sinful lips.

I hummed in appreciation as she applied just a bit more pressure to my pussy, still trying to get more, more, more from her.

"So greedy this morning, siúcra." I was. I wanted a distraction, and she offered me the best kind.

"Please, Molly," I begged, not even caring how desperate I sounded.

"What do you want?" she asked breathlessly in my ear. "Tell me."

"More."

"More what? Tell me exactly what you want me to do to this sweet pussy."

"I want your fingers deep inside of me while you suck on my clit," I said.

"Your wish is my command," she growled, spinning me and pushing me up against the shower wall. I sucked in a shocked gasp, her breath already tickling my cunt. With no preamble, she dove right in, giving me exactly what I asked for.

I reached down, gripping her wet hair with both hands as I rode her face and fingers. I peeked down to see that she was also touching herself, and I could feel her soft moans against me, the vibrations adding to my pleasure.

Within minutes, Molly was groaning her orgasm, sending me over into my own. We both stayed there for a minute, fighting the light-headedness. Molly pressed a gentle kiss to my thigh, before rising and giving me a passionate kiss. I knew she was distracting me on purpose, and I was grateful for it. I no longer worried about Nathan or my dad. I smiled against her lips.

"I love you," I whispered. My eyes popped open, and panic filled me. I hadn't meant to say that, and I knew it was too early. She was going to freak out.

She pulled back just the slightest and gazed into my eyes. "Did you just say what I think you said?" When I didn't respond, just stared at her with wide eyes, she chuckled and a beautiful smile lit up her face. "I love you too, siúcra."

Instead of replying, I leaned in and brushed my lips against hers. I poured everything I felt for her into that kiss. She gave as good as she got, and we were breathless by the time we pulled apart.

I rested my forehead against hers, enjoying the closeness. "I've never met anyone like you before. You make me want to be my best self, but you never judge me even when I'm not," I told her sincerely.

I realized in that moment I wanted to share everything with her. Just as I opened my mouth, my phone alarm went off on the bathroom counter. I sighed deeply before pulling away from her.

"Time to get up," I teased, seeing as we were already awake and moving about, giving her another quick kiss.

"You have to work today?"

"Unfortunately, yes, but Savannah is in today too, so I'm going to firm up some plans with her for our triple date."

"Can I come in with you? I want to chat with her about doing a tattoo for me."

Surprise flickered through me, but I smiled in delight. I was so down for her to get another tattoo. "Want your tight pretty nipples pierced while you're there?" I asked, pinching them in a tight grasp, heat flooding me when she gasped against me.

"Yes," she moaned.

"Really? 'Cause it's going to hurt more than this," I purred, squeezing even harder.

"Please," she whispered. I looked down to find her shifting her hips forward, seeking friction to ease the ache I started inside her.

"Okay, doll. I'll give you what you want. But not yet." I pulled away from her, releasing her hard buds, making her gasp again.

"Are you leaving me hanging?" she growled.

"Just for now, love. We can continue this when I get some needles involved."

Her eyebrows shot up to her hairline, and a blush had risen to those pretty cheeks.

"You mean, in your shop?"

"Yes. Now if you get your tight little ass moving, we can get there before everyone else and have some fun."

I slapped her ass as I stepped out of the shower. She followed me a minute later, and we were both rushing to get ready so we could have some more fun. The blush stayed on her face the whole time, and I knew she was just as excited about what we were about to do as I was.

We got to the shop twenty minutes before the opener was supposed to get there. I knew Savannah was opening, so if she walked in on anything, it wouldn't be a big deal, but I didn't tell Molly that. We went back to my station, and I pulled the privacy curtain around us, just in case.

"Take off your clothes," I ordered while I sterilized my station. She did as I told her, not questioning why she needed her bottoms off too. "Sit down and spread your legs for me."

She once again followed orders as I got my gloves on and prepped the needle and her jewelry. I looked down at her to find her dripping onto my table as she bit her lip in anticipation.

"Fuck. You have such a pretty cunt," I whispered before leaning in to give her a heated kiss. I pulled back and my mouth immediately went to her chest. I flicked both nipples with my tongue before pulling back and blowing cool air on them. She moaned, making me delight in the fact that I could make her so excited from barely touching her. I went down farther and swiped my tongue through the folds of her pussy a few times. Her hands immediately gripped my hair, pulling me tight against her. I gave her one more lick before I stood. She was blushing more furiously now and panting. She looked ready to strangle me.

Before she knew what I was doing, I swiped an alcohol swab against her nipples, making her gasp in surprise. "Put your fingers on your clit, Molly." She did, immediately moaning as they swirled around rapidly. "Slow down, love. We want this to last at least until the needles are through."

Her eyes were closed and her head tilted back as I clamped the first nipple, and she sighed in pleasure. "Keep your fingers moving," I warned as I pushed the needle through, knowing that the movements from her hand would distract her and hopefully make this a more pleasant experience for her. She whimpered, whether in pain, pleasure, or both I wasn't sure. I put the jewelry in as quickly as I could and then taped a bandage over it.

"Ready for the second one?" I asked. When she nodded, I leaned in, giving her another sloppy kiss. She moaned against my mouth and as soon as I pulled back I clamped her other nipple. Her fingers were moving faster now and I wasn't sure if she was close or if it was more to distract herself. Either way, the sight was more than distracting, and I had to concentrate to make sure I pierced it correctly. I tore my eyes away from her pussy and focused on the task at hand. Within seconds I had the next needle through and the jewelry on. She opened her eyes then, a couple of tears falling, but her eyes were heated on mine. She looked down at her nipple before I put the bandage over it, and as soon as I was finished, I tore the gloves off and dropped to my knees in front of her. My fingers replaced hers, diving deep between her folds, and my lips strongly latched on to her clit. She exploded, pulsing around my fingers and flooding my mouth. As soon as she finished groaning her release and riding against me, I heard the front door chime. Molly froze as her horrified gaze met mine.

Chapter 14

Anna

"Good morning!" Savannah shouted as she came in, shuffling around at the front desk.

"Hey, babe!" I shouted back as normally as I could, smiling up at Molly.

"What are you doing here so early? And why do you have the curtain drawn?" she asked.

"I was just giving Molly another piercing," I replied to her. "Put your clothes back on and meet us out front," I whispered to Molly, biting down gently on her earlobe, making her sharply inhale.

As soon as she got off the table, I quickly sanitized everything and then made my way out to Savannah. She was sitting at the desk waiting for the computer to boot up and looking over the schedule for the day.

"Damn, we're slow today. What did Molly get pierced?"

"Her chest," I replied honestly. It was the only way to explain why I had the curtain drawn.

"Anna!" Molly exclaimed, clearly embarrassed that I told her.

"It's no big deal, babe. I pierced Savannah's a couple years ago."

"She's right. It hurt like a bitch too. How did yours feel?" she asked.

"Oh, just wonderful," Molly replied, a fierce blush rising, making me almost laugh out loud. Before Savannah could comment, Molly quickly changed the subject. "I'm actually glad you're here. I wanted to see if you'd be willing to do a tattoo for me?"

Savannah's eyes lit up and I could tell she was excited about the prospect. She loved tattooing, and I knew it would probably end up being a big bonding moment between the two of them.

"Yes, I would love to! Do you have any others besides the one on your chest?"

"Nope. I'm new to the whole tattoo thing. I only got this one like a year ago."

If it was possible, Savannah looked even more excited. She loved working with a blank canvas. She rubbed her palms together as she smiled.

"What did you have in mind?"

"Well, I want two..." This woman was surprising me on all fronts today. "The first one would be super small, just an acupuncture needle behind my ear. The second one I want is the outline of Ireland with a simple compass over it. I was thinking that one could go on my forearm if you think it will fit there?"

They continued talking over specifics, and I left them to it as I looked at the schedule. Savannah was right, it really was dead. I had only one appointment at noon and then the rest of my day was open. Granted, most people didn't book appointments for piercings, they usually just walked in, but still.

"So, do you want to do it now? I don't have anything until one," Savannah asked.

"As much as I would love to, I don't think my body can handle any more needles today," Molly said, grimacing. I could tell then that she was hurting pretty bad.

Savannah nodded sympathetically. "I had forgotten about that. Yeah, you would not want to get a tattoo right now." After another few minutes of chatting, she put her on the books for three weeks out.

"I'm going to get going, siúcra. Text me." Molly leaned over the counter and gave me a quick kiss. "Thanks for the piercings."

"Sure thing, doll," I drawled. "I'll make sure to check on them later." I gave her a saucy wink, making her blush. She waved at me and Savannah before walking out.

"So what did you guys really do back there?" Savannah asked as soon as Molly was out the door.

"What are you talking about? I just pierced her nipples," I said innocently.

"You are so full of shit. And since when are you shy about giving me all the dirty details? I thought you thought that I lived for them."

"You don't?" I asked with mock shock, making her roll her eyes. "Well, there might've been some dirtiness that ensued."

She laughed, plopping down on the couch in the front room. Since we didn't have anything for a while, we just hung out. Jared walked in ten minutes later.

He walked past my station before stopping abruptly. "Do I smell pussy?" he asked. My face turned beet red as I turned shocked eyes to Savannah. She looked like she was about to bust out laughing. I shook my head at her, giving her the death stare, just daring her to say anything.

"Jared, you're such a perv. Why do you think you smell vagina everywhere? It's probably coming from your clothes," I lied my ass off, hoping he wouldn't further investigate my station. He looked back at me, contemplating, before nodding like he realized it probably was coming from him and headed back to his station.

"Don't say 'vagina.' It weirds me out," he yelled when he got there.

Savannah chuckled under her breath and I shot her a dirty look. "So, do we have any plans for the triple yet?" I asked.

"Well, I was thinking maybe we could have dinner and then do a First Friday art walk?"

"Oh, that sounds fun. I've never done one before."

"Me neither, but there's one coming up soon."

"That sounds perfect. I'll text Molly to make sure she isn't working that night. Have you guys found your outfits yet?" I asked.

"Not yet. We're going tonight after work. Charlie has the day off. I can't wait to find something absolutely absurd for him to wear. Did you guys find some good stuff?"

"Bitch, we found the best outfits. We're going to look so ridiculous. And we had so much fun picking them out."

All of a sudden, she gave me a strange look. She reached over to pull something out of my hair. "What the fuck is in your hair, and why isn't it coming out?"

I laughed loudly at that. "It's paint."

"Paint?" she asked.

"Yeah. That was the second half of our date last night."

"What? To bathe in it?"

"Well, no. We were painting each other and then a paint war ensued, which led to multiple dirty acts."

Her eyebrows rose in surprise. I hadn't told her about that part when she helped me plan the surprise date. "I gotta give you points for creativity."

As we sat there chatting, I started getting chills up the back of my neck. I turned around, expecting to see someone at the window, but there was no one there. I shivered.

"What is it?" Savannah asked.

I shook my head, turning back to her. "It's nothing. I just got a little chilly is all," I lied. I couldn't shake the feeling that someone was watching me. I thought of my dream from the previous night, and another shiver worked its way up my spine. I looked out the windows one more time, just to double-check that no one was there, but I didn't see anyone. I was probably just being paranoid, but the feeling made me antsy.

Luckily, at that point, a girl walked in wanting her lip pierced. Grateful for the distraction, and something to do to shake my restlessness, I led her back to my station right away.

Someone there or not, I thought it was time to take a trip to the shooting range.

After work, I went straight to the gun range. Luckily, since I had my concealed carry, I already had my weapon with me. This place also had ammo that you could buy, as well as ear and eye protection for rent. I had a membership, so I came here pretty often, although no one really knew.

I always felt the need to be prepared in case my past decided to sneak up on me, and whenever I got a bad feeling, or felt unnecessarily paranoid, I made a trip here. I hadn't been in a while, but as I walked in, I inhaled the smell of metal and gunpowder and smiled, feeling in my element.

"Anna. Haven't seen you here in an age. How you doin', darlin'?"

"Good, Frank. How have you been?" I asked the Southern, middle-aged man who owned the place. He was almost always here, and even though he didn't like anyone to know, he was a big teddy bear.

"The ulcer has been acting up again, so I've had to lay off all my favorite spicy foods, but good other than that. Just missed your pretty face around here."

I smiled at him. "Aww, Frank, I missed your pretty face too," I told him, earning a chuckle.

"You need everything you normally do, doll?"

"Yes, sir."

Ten minutes later, I was in my favorite stall. There was no one here, just how I liked it. I put on my earmuffs and protective eye goggles and got into stance before loading my gun. I took a deep breath in and unloaded the full clip into the target in front of me. When the smoke cleared, I took a look at my handiwork and smiled. It made me feel calmer when I knew that I could protect myself and those I loved if need be. I had the proof right here in front of me.

I got lost in the feeling, only paying attention to how the comforting weight of the gun and the warm metal felt in my hands, the jolt as I fired and it traveled down my arm, the smell of gunpowder and smoke.

Forty-five minutes and lots of ammo later, I walked out feeling much calmer, and no longer felt like I was being watched.

Chapter 15

Molly

I drove home after getting my nipples pierced. I was exhausted, and my tits were throbbing. The experience itself had been pretty pleasurable, considering the way it went down, but now, with the way my breasts were hurting, I was not a happy camper.

I walked in, tossing my keys on the table by the door, and headed straight to the bedroom and stripped off my clothes from yesterday, making sure to take extra care while removing my shirt. I decided to take a shower to wash my new piercings even though I had taken one not even an hour prior, but I figured the steam would also clear my foggy head.

I looked in the mirror, laughing as I eyed the bandages over my breasts. They helped, but they definitely weren't the most flattering things I'd ever had covering my nipples. I removed them as gently as I could, but it still felt like the tape was pulling my skin right off.

Once I got them off, I looked in the mirror again, smiling at what I saw. I had always wanted my tits pierced, but I had been too nervous to get them done. I finally felt comfortable enough with Anna, and I knew that she would make it as painless as possible, which she had obviously accomplished. I didn't have anything fancy in them, just plain silver barbells, but I loved how they looked, and I was excited to get some fun jewelry once they'd healed.

I hopped in the shower and gently washed my breasts with antibacterial soap. They were extremely tender, so it took me a few minutes to get the job done, but I was glad I decided to do it so I could get all the stickiness from the tape off.

When I finished, I dressed in my robe, wanting to be comfy and really not wanting to put regular clothes on. Plus the robe gave my girls plenty of room to breathe. I was grateful I had the next couple days off so I could let them heal. I knew it was going to be a bitch going back into work with these, and I would have to be careful how I moved around.

I picked up my phone, thinking I should probably phone home. I hadn't talked to my parents all week, and I missed them. Mam answered on the second ring.

"Hello," she practically yelled into the phone.

"Hey, Mamaí."

"Oh, iníon," she always called me, which translated to "daughter." "It's so good to hear from you, darling. How are you?"

"I'm good. I met someone," I told her straightaway, too excited to wait.

"Oh my goodness, you did? When can we meet her?" I laughed out loud. My mother always wanted to meet my girlfriends right away. It was like having another daughter, she said.

"Soon, Mam. I'll check with her and see if we can make the drive to Colorado Springs soon."

"What's her name? Tell me all about my new daughter," she said, making me laugh again. I had called it.

"Her name is Anna. We met at a yoga class. She's a piercer at a tattoo shop. She's loud and crass, but very sweet and funny."

"Oh, honey, that's so good to hear. She's a piercer? Has she pierced you yet, Molly Claire?" I cringed at my mother's tone and the fact that she used my first and middle name together.

"Maybe?" I said, feeling a blush rising to my cheeks, and it got worse when I thought of what she pierced that morning, not to mention the way it was done.

I heard her sigh and thought that I could feel the phone rumble with the force of it. "What did she pierce?"

"Which time?" I asked, before I could stop myself. I immediately rolled my eyes and smacked myself in the forehead.

"Molly!" she exclaimed, making me flinch.

"Well, when did you meet her?" she asked, seemingly ready to move on to another topic, for which I was grateful. I really didn't think my mam would be pleased to know that Anna had put needles through my nipples.

"A couple weeks ago?"

"And you're just now telling me about it? I talked to you a week ago, iníon," she reprimanded, and I wasn't surprised. If she had her way, I would tell her every single detail of my life the moment it happened.

"I know, but I don't like to jinx anything, Mamaí, so I don't usually tell you until I'm pretty sure it's going to turn into something."

"So, it's turning into something serious?" Mam lived for my love life.

"Well, she did tell me she loved me this morning," I replied quietly, with a smile in my voice.

She squealed into the phone. Literally squealed. "Oh, darling. I'm so happy for you. You have to bring her down now. How about this weekend?"

"Mam, I haven't even talked to her about it yet. We also have a triple date with her friends soon so it might be a couple weekends before we're able to make it down." She sighed into the phone, likely about to tell me to come down anyway, but I spoke up before she could do that.

"Next time I see her, though, I'll ask her about it, and we will set a date to come down to see you and Daidí."

"Well, I guess that's the best I'm going to get then," she relented, making me chuckle.

"How's Da doing?"

"Oh, you know him. He's still playing soccer with his men's league every week, even though his knees give him constant trouble."

"Are they getting worse?" I asked, concerned. My father had multiple knee injuries when he was younger, courtesy of all the sports he played. When I lived near my parents, I would do acupuncture on his knees weekly, which really seemed to help, but he was stubborn and didn't want to see anyone else other than me.

"A little bit. I keep telling him to go to the doctor, but you know how much he loves doing that kind of thing." I nodded, 'cause I knew exactly how he was. "Other than that, though, he's doing well. He keeps telling me that he's thinking of finally retiring, but I think he's full of shit. He loves working way too much. Not to mention that he's been saying the same thing for a year, and still has made no move toward doing it."

I laughed out loud then, because this was a conversation I had with her every time we talked. I knew my dad would stop working eventually, but I think when it did finally happen, it would not be how either of them thought. My mam had been retired for a while now, and loved having the house to herself. She filled her days with gardening, crafting, and housework of any kind, mainly redecorating and rearranging. Every time I went to their house, at least one room was completely flipped around. I knew she loved my dad too, but she really enjoyed having all that time to herself. When he did retire, there would be a big adjustment period for them both.

"It'll happen when he's ready, Mam. How's your garden coming along?"

"The fucking deer keep eating all my flowers," she complained, making me laugh again. Yet another thing she talked about every year. They had a lot of deer in Colorado Springs, and she had problems with them whenever she planted new flowers. She put a spray on them, but they still ate them, albeit somewhat less frequently than without the spray, but she hated them wrecking all of her hard work. Secretly, I don't think that she minded too much. It kept her busy, and she loved working outside. Honestly, if she had her way, she would be outside all the time.

"Of course they do. Which flowers did they eat this time?"

"My tulips. I know better, but they're just so pretty that I can never resist. They lasted about three days before those little fuckers came through."

She and I continued chatting for about twenty minutes, which usually happened whenever I called her. Not much had changed in a week, but we missed each other and found stuff to talk about.

"Okay, Mam. Well, I'll let you get back to your day. Plant something else that the deer don't like this time. I also expect some fresh tomatoes when I come down, so make sure to save some for me."

"I will, darling. I love you, and give my new daughter a nice big hug for me."

"Will do. Love you too, and tell Da that I love him and miss him too."

We hung up, and I decided to spend the remainder of my day resting. Despite sleeping super well the night before with Anna, I woke earlier than I usually did, probably because I had sensed when she had gotten out of bed. We had also been up late the night before doing very active things. I collapsed onto my mattress with my heating pad, and I turned my TV and promptly fell asleep.

The next few days passed by quickly. Anna and I were able to get together during the nights, usually after one or both of us had to work. We switched off between staying at her place and mine, developing our own routine. We made love frequently, more so than I think either of us had in any previous relationship, but I couldn't help it, I just couldn't keep my hands or mouth off of her, and it seemed that she felt the same way about me.

"So, I have plans with the girls tomorrow," she told me before bed one night.

"Oh, fun. What are you ladies going to do?"

"We're just going to grab lunch, and then go to Fascinations."

"What is that?"

"It's a sex shop. We like to go there fairly regularly. Sometimes we get a bunch of stuff, other times we just browse and laugh at the ridiculousness we find."

"Are you going to get something fun for us?" I asked.

"I'm not sure yet. Any requests?"

"How about some flavored massage oil?"

"I like the sound of that," she murmured against my skin, before kissing my neck softly.

"And you know how I always love some lingerie to showcase your sexy body."

"Also doable," she agreed, snuggling even closer to me in bed.

Within minutes, we were sound asleep.

The next day, I was at work, just finishing up my last group of clients for the day. The next acupuncturist had already walked in the door and was getting ready for their shift. Usually, when the next shift came in, the new arrival would work on any people who came in after their shift started, and the first acupuncturist finished up with everybody they had been working on before leaving for the day.

I was in the office, finishing up my client notes for the day when my phone rang. I looked down to see that Anna was calling, which was strange since she had said she would be hanging out with the girls today.

"Hey, siúcra. Everything okay?"

"Molly? It's Savannah."

"What's going on? Is everything okay? Where's Anna?" I knew I was asking a lot of questions, but I was already nervous seeing Anna calling me, and when I heard Savannah's voice, I knew something was going on.

"We just drove Anna to the emergency room."

Chapter 16

Anna

The girls and I started at The Matador for lunch. They had good Mexican food, and more importantly, drinks. It had been a while since the three of us had spent a day together, and I was really looking forward to it.

"So, I kind of have some news," Savannah told us while we waited for our food.

"Well, don't keep us in suspense. What is it?" I asked.

"I'm getting my IUD taken out next week."

"Oh my *God*!" I screamed, not caring when several people looked over at me.

"You guys are going to start trying?" Lauren asked. At Savannah's nod, we all started clapping, exclaiming, and hugging. We didn't care that we were being obnoxious and that we were in public. We were being *those* girls, and we did not give two shits.

"That is so exciting," I said. "When did you guys decide this?"

"Well, we started talking about it around two months ago. Charlie was actually the one to bring it up, and ever since he mentioned it, I haven't been able to stop thinking about it. At first, I was really nervous about the prospect. I mean it's no secret that I don't have the best parents in the world, but after I told Charlie about my fears, he helped me to see that I am nothing like my family, and that I would be a wonderful mother. I had a yearly physical scheduled already, so we decided that I would just get it taken out then."

"I call godmother!" I shouted.

"You *bitch*!" Lauren exclaimed, staring at me incredulously.

Savannah laughed at us. "How do either of you know it won't be someone else?"

"Bitch, please. We're like your only friends," I said, rolling my eyes.

"You know what? Just for that, I'm picking Lauren."

"*Yes*!" Lauren shouted victoriously.

"No fair! You know it's true," I said with a pout.

Our food came then, and we all dug in. Ten minutes into the meal, chills ran down the back of my neck. I had that feeling again that someone was watching me. Thinking back, though, I remembered that I'd had another nightmare about Nathan the night before, and I chalked it up to that.

"So, what now? Pedicures?" Lauren asked as we finished up our drinks and meal.

"Oh God. Yes, please. I need one so bad," Savannah said.

I gave a thumbs-up as I downed the rest of my drink. We paid the bill and decided to walk to the closest nail salon. It was, after all, only a few blocks away.

When we were only a block away from the salon, I felt the hairs stand on end all over my body. I gasped, stopping in the middle of the sidewalk. My heart started beating faster, and I had the sensation that I was underwater, like I couldn't get any air into my lungs no matter how fast I was breathing.

"Anna? Are you okay?" I barely heard Lauren ask me.

I could've sworn someone was watching me. Closely. I swung

around, my gaze flying to every person I could see. There were a lot of people out, but I didn't see anyone I knew. My breath was coming faster, and my chest felt like it was ready to burst. I stuck a hand against my sternum, trying to rub away the pain.

"My chest hurts," I panicked.

"Jesus, Anna. You're white as a ghost," Savannah said, and I vaguely realized she sounded fairly concerned. Black spots danced in my vision, and before I knew what was happening, everything went dark.

I woke up, God knows how long after, in a hospital bed. As soon as my eyes opened, the girls were immediately at my side.

"Anna, how are you feeling?" Lauren asked, sounding beyond relieved.

"Confused. What the hell happened?" I felt so fuzzy.

"We were heading to the nail salon when you started hyperventilating and talking about your chest hurting. A minute later you passed out, so we called an ambulance. You've been out for about an hour. They checked you out and said everything was fine. They think you had a panic attack," Savannah explained.

Everything came rushing back to me, and my anxiety spiked again. I could hear the heart monitor going crazy, and I was breathing quicker again.

"Anna, you're safe. Just calm down," Lauren soothed, grabbing my hand and rubbing my back in gentle circles. It helped marginally, but I still felt extremely amped up. "Take some deep breaths with me. Let's do some yogic breathing. Long inhales through the nose…" I followed her command, breathing with her. "Long exhale through the nose. Feel the constriction in the back of your throat. Concentrate on that," she guided me.

After a couple of breaths, I was able to focus on the wavelike sound of our breathing. It took a few minutes, but I finally settled, and I noticed the heart monitor had toned down as well.

Before I was able to explain, or ask more questions, the door flew open, revealing a panicked and frazzled-looking Molly.

"Siúcra, are you okay? What happened?" She rushed over to me, running her fingers over my cheek.

"I'm fine, Molly. Apparently I had a panic attack," I told her as soothingly as I could. I felt even more calm as soon as I saw her face.

I watched relief flicker over her features, but her face was still etched in concern. "I was so worried when Savannah called me. Do you know what caused it? Weren't you guys just having a relaxing girls' day?"

I looked at all of the ladies surrounding me, and my heart started racing again. It was time to tell them everything. Not telling them could put them in danger, and it was time that I finally faced my past, considering that I was pretty sure it was coming for me.

"I need to tell you all something. Something big." I took a deep breath, feeling my anxiety mounting again.

"Hold on. Before you do, I'm just going to put some acupuncture needles in your ears," Molly quickly interrupted. My guess was that she felt how badly I needed a reprieve from my anxiety. She pulled out a couple of packages of needles from her purse, quickly inserted five needles in both ears, and for the first time since I woke up, I was able to take a true full deep breath. I smiled at her gratefully before I started in on my story.

"I grew up in Georgia..." Just with those words, I could already feel my accent popping out slightly. I worked so hard to get rid of it, but it tended to come out when I was very upset, or when I started thinking about my hometown or my past. I took another deep breath.

"I was raised extremely religious. We were Jehovah's Witnesses."

I heard one of the girls inhale, I thought it might've been Savannah, but whether it was from me *finally* talking about my past, or the fact that I was raised in such a strict religion, I had no idea.

"My father was a ministerial servant. They're basically the equivalent of a deacon. He eventually wanted to be an elder, and was actually getting close to gaining that title. Then my mom got sick, and everything was put on the backburner. She had breast cancer, but they didn't catch it until it was too late. She went downhill fast, and we lost her three months later. I was thirteen."

I paused, focusing on the throbbing of the needles in my ears, instead of the captivated and devastated gazes of my loved ones or the pinpricks of hot tears gathering behind my eyes. Once I felt like I wasn't going to start bawling, I continued.

"My dad threw himself back into his work with the church, and even though he didn't mean to, I was pretty neglected. We went on like that for a few years before he met a woman in our church. They started dating, and while I was happy that he found someone, Carol never really seemed to like me. Either way, the church was happy for them and approved of the marriage. Being religious, they weren't able to live together before they got married, so things moved pretty quickly. Before I knew it, my world had changed again, and I had a new *mother*...and a new stepbrother."

As much as they needed to know, I literally had to force the words past my lips. I took another deep breath, and told myself that telling this story couldn't hurt me.

"At first, I really liked Nathan," I said, almost choking on his name. "We used to hang out quite a bit. He never really knew his dad, and he didn't have any other siblings, and we were the same age, so I think we both felt like we could make each other a little less lonely. As we got older, we started feeling rebellious, as all teenagers do, especially in religious households. What was originally us just innocently hanging out, eventually turned into us breaking the rules. It started one night when we were bored and decided to sneak out of the house. We didn't even do anything bad that time, just went to hang out at the park down the street, but the act of doing something we weren't supposed to became almost irresistible. By this time, we were fifteen. We did the sneaking-out thing pretty often for a while before it became boring. Our next rebellion was drinking. I don't know where Nathan got it from, but one night he knocked on my bedroom door with a bottle of tequila. That one we kept up for a while, sometimes drinking in one of our rooms, sometimes sneaking out to drink. Our parents were so wrapped up in each other that they didn't even notice anything was wrong.

"As you probably guessed, we liked each other. We flirted with each other plenty, but us being raised so strictly, we were also newbies in this too. I could tell Nathan wanted to add having sex to our 'rebellion list,' but that was one thing that I didn't want to rush into, or to do just because we wanted to do something bad. He kissed me one night, and as much as I liked it, I told him I wasn't ready. I knew he wasn't happy about it, but he left it alone for a while. Now that I think back on it, I want to say he was even MIA for a couple days after I told him. He was still around the house, but he stopped coming by my room, and there was no more sneaking out or drinking with me.

"Then one night, maybe a week or two later, he knocked on my door at three in the morning. I had been dead asleep, and was confused, thinking something must have been wrong. When I opened the door, he swayed on the threshold, telling me how pretty I was. I knew then that he had been drinking, more than we ever had before. I had seen him drunk, but not like this. He stumbled into my room, and before I knew what was happening, he was kissing me. At first I was relieved because I thought he had been pissed at me for not wanting to go fast with him, but here he was, kissing me. That relief quickly turned to dread. Things were progressing quickly, his hand was under my shirt and he was guiding me toward the bed. I tried pulling away from him, but he didn't let me get very far.

When I finally got my mouth free of his, I told him to stop and that he was moving too fast for me. He shushed me and attacked my mouth again. I kept pushing him away, but nothing was working. Not long after, he had me on the bed, and I'm sure you can figure out the rest. Afterward, I remember I had tears streaming down my cheeks, and I was just lying in my bed not able to comprehend what happened. He leaned over me, the coldest look in his eyes, and told me that if I ever told anyone what happened that he would kill me."

I whispered the last part, still unable to comprehend the change that happened in Nathan. I heard Lauren gasp, and when I finally looked up, meeting all of their gazes, I saw tears in all of their eyes. I quickly looked back down at my hands, unable to take their sympathy. Molly reached over and grasped my hand tightly in hers. I squeezed back gratefully.

"It happened a few more times over the next year. He was always extremely drunk when it occurred. By the third time, I couldn't take it anymore. I told my father what happened." The next words were so hard to get out, but I made myself spit them out.

"He didn't believe me. He thought that I was trying to get attention and that I was acting out because he got married. He said that I needed to get it together and straighten up, because the church would look poorly on him and never let him become an elder if he couldn't even control his own daughter."

"No," Molly said quietly, shaking her head, tears streaming down her face. "How could he?" Her cheeks were blazing red, and although she was crying, there was a fire in her eyes that said she wanted to burn the world down for me, and everyone who ever hurt me would be first.

"I realized the other day that I think all of that really affected my sexual orientation, honestly. I think I denied what I was for so long because I was taught that I would go to hell if I ever felt that way about a woman. Then, if that shit hadn't happened with Nathan, I would probably be bisexual, but I've never felt comfortable with any man, especially romantically. Not since him.

"Anyway, I ran away the day after I told my dad. I had just turned sixteen. When I left, though, all I could hear was Nathan's voice in my head and telling me, 'Hannah, I'll kill you if you tell anyone.'"

"Your real name is Hannah?" Savannah whispered.

"Out of all of that, that's what you latched on to?" I asked, laughing despite myself.

"Well, you just really don't seem like a 'Hannah' to me," she replied, a slight smile in her voice.

"I've changed a lot since I was Hannah. That name definitely doesn't fit me anymore. Anyway, I didn't want anyone to find me, so I changed my name as soon as I left. I got a gun as soon as I could, carrying one illegally until I could get my concealed carry. I've known how to shoot for years, just in case Nathan comes to find me. There was such a deadness in his eyes when he told me that I believe that he will stick to his promise. And I think he's finally found me. I keep feeling someone watching me. That's why I had a panic attack today. I think he was there. I think he's waiting to make his move."

Dread coiled tightly in my stomach at the thought of what he would do to me.

"Anna, er, Hannah," Lauren said awkwardly, making me flinch.

"Oh God. Please don't ever call me that." I grimaced.

"Sorry, babe. Anna, are you sure you felt someone watching you?"

"I think so. When I first noticed it, I had literally just dreamt about him the night before, so I originally thought that I was being paranoid because of that, but today, I could've sworn I felt someone watching me. I looked around, and I didn't see him, but there were a lot of people on the street today."

"Have you ever felt like this before?" Molly asked.

"Sometimes when I dream about him I will get a little paranoid, but I've never gotten this strong of a feeling before. Not to mention that the dream that I had about him felt like a premonition, and that scares the ever loving shit out of me," I admitted, tears finally making their appearance. I quickly swatted them away, not wanting anyone to see my weakness.

"Siúcra, look at me." I reluctantly met her gaze. "I'm not going to let anything happen to you. Not that you need me to look after you, because you are the strongest, bravest person I know, but if he tries to come for you, I will tear him apart," Molly seethed.

My eyes widened in surprise. I never thought Molly to be the violent type, but here she was, threatening to fuck someone up for me. More tears welled in my eyes. I hadn't had someone in my corner like this in a long time.

Of course Lauren and Savannah were always there for me, and I could even see them nodding in agreement and support behind her, but to have them accept what I told them without question, and to be this upset for me, made me wish that I had gotten this kind of a reaction when I had told my dad. And to wish for my mom, because she would've been the same way. I smiled when I realized that Molly was quite a bit like my mother.

"I love you," I told her without reservation this time.

"I love you too, siúcra. God help anyone who tries to take you from me."

Chapter 17

Molly

A week after Anna's panic attack, we decided to make a trip to Colorado Springs to visit my folks. I was originally going to wait until after our triple date to bring her home, but as soon as I told Anna about it, she was very excited and wanted to go on our next days off. My mam was ecstatic; Da didn't really care as long as she was good to me and I was happy.

I was in the driver's seat, making the hour and a half drive to the Springs, while Anna was on her phone, constantly changing the music station. I swear to God, she had the worst case of music ADD I had ever seen. I smiled fondly at her. Most people might find her to be a bit much, but not me. Her craziness was partly why I was so in love with her.

We had decided to spend the night for a couple reasons. First, the drive was a *bitch,* and I really hated going there and back all in the same day. Even though it was only one and a half to two hours, there was always so much traffic, and they had been doing construction from Castle Rock to Monument for years. Secondly, my mam would flip her shit if we didn't. She wanted to get to know her "new daughter" and apparently she needed at least two days to accomplish that.

As we crossed over into Colorado Springs, Anna started getting fidgety. She was twirling her hair around her finger and bouncing her knee up and down.

"You nervous?" I asked.

"No, I'm totally fine," she lied.

"Really? 'Cause I'm pretty sure with how much your foot is moving I'm either going to have an orgasm or the car is going to fall apart from everything being shaken loose," I teased.

She rolled her eyes, but smiled at me, stilling her foot. "I guess I am a little bit. I've never met a significant other's parents before, not to mention that I don't really have parents anymore, so I don't know how I should interact with them."

"Siúcra, my parents are going to love you. Just be yourself. They are not uptight in the least. I'm sure my mam already likes you more than me, and she doesn't even know you yet."

She took a deep breath, nodding as I exited on Woodman Road. I smiled. This was my hometown (basically), and it always felt welcoming and homey whenever I was here. I turned down my parents' street and looked over at Anna. She was taking everything in with wide eyes. Colorado Springs was much prettier than Denver in my opinion. It was right up against the mountains so there was a lot more nature around. More trees, more mountains, more animals. But then again, I'd never been a big city girl. I had only moved to Denver to go to acupuncture school.

"Have you been here before?" I asked her.

"No. Castle Rock is the closest I've been. It's gorgeous here."

"Just wait 'til you see all the deer at my parents' house."

"They have *deer*?" she squealed excitedly, making me chuckle as I pulled into the driveway. Before I even put the car into park, my mother was opening the door and walking toward us, not even waiting for us to get out of the vehicle. She had Anna's door open before she even had her seat belt off. I rolled my eyes and smiled at her excitement. It had been a while since she had met any of my girlfriends.

"Oh, Anna dear. It's so good to meet you!" she exclaimed, pulling her into a tight hug. "I'm so glad you were able to come down so soon to see us. Molly wanted to wait a few weeks. How ridiculous is that?" she rambled, sticking that nice little guilt trip on the end there.

"Cara, it's so nice to meet you too," Anna said, hugging her back just as tightly. I had told Anna that my parents didn't like formality and would not appreciate being called by their last name, O'Malley. My mam absolutely beamed at me over Anna's shoulder.

"Why don't you come in, dear? I have lunch on the stove," she said, grasping her hand and dragging her into the house. I grabbed our things, and quickly dropped them off in my room before joining them in the kitchen.

I wrapped my mam in a hug from behind as she stirred something in one of the pans. "Hi Mamaí. I've missed you," I said as she turned around to give me a real hug.

"Oh, iníon. I've missed you too." I loved Mam hugs. They were the best. As I broke away from her, I looked over at Anna, seeing a sad smile on her face. "Your father should be down in a minute. I made him put on clean clothes since we have company." I laughed at that. My da wasn't always great about remembering to do stuff like basic cleanliness, but that's why he had my mother to remind him.

"What's for lunch, Mam?" I asked.

"Just stew and soda bread, darling."

I barely contained my excitement. This was one of my favorite family meals. We had the best soda bread recipe ever. Of course every Irish family thought that because every family's recipe was different with the exception of a few ingredients.

"Yum!" I exclaimed, making Mam smile. She knew that it was one of my favorites and she cooked it whenever I was down. Of course, the stew was usually cooked with meat, but she never added that since I was a vegetarian.

My father walked in a moment later. His face broke out in a huge smile as soon as he saw me. I ran up to him and swung my arms around him. "Daidí, it's so good to see you."

"You too, a stór," he replied. That had been his nickname for me since before I could remember. It translated to "my treasure." "Ah, you must be Anna," he said, shaking Anna's hand politely. He wasn't much of a hugger unless he knew you really well. "Cara here hasn't stopped gushing about you coming down for days."

"Oh, Liam. That's not true," Mam said, slapping his arm lightly as she blushed furiously. Obviously that was where I got that particular trait.

"Thank you both so much for having me come down. I've really been looking forward to meeting you," Anna jumped in.

"Anytime, Anna dear. Would you like anything to drink? Water, wine, beer?"

"Is anyone else drinking?" she asked, clearly not wanting to be the only one.

"Babe, we're Irish. We drink with almost every meal," I teased, grabbing us each a Guinness from out of the fridge. It was a staple in this house, something that we never went without. Pretty typical, I know, but we loved it. My parents both had fairly thick accents and mine got thicker whenever I was around them.

Lunch was ready soon after, and I dug in, not even caring that I probably looked like I hadn't eaten in a week. It always comforted me, and made me feel at home. Anna was eating with just as much gusto beside me, exclaiming how good it was. Mam positively glowed at the praise.

After lunch, we all went out on the patio, enjoying the sun and the slightly cool breeze. Fall would be here soon, and I was so looking forward to it. It was my favorite season by far, and then the holidays weren't far behind. I was really excited to share that all with Anna.

"Oh my God, there's a deer!" Anna exclaimed loudly, almost scaring off the poor thing.

"She's been coming around here quite a bit lately. Her babies should be right behind her," Mam told her. "I think she's the main one that's been eating my flowers."

A moment later, her two babies made their way into the yard. "They are the cutest things I've ever seen," Anna said, awed. "I've never seen any babies in person."

"They're pretty precious," I said, "just be careful around the mama. She'll be very protective over them, so don't get too close."

She nodded absently, not taking her eyes off the little family. My parents both smiled at me, enjoying her awe. It was easy to get used to, so it was nice having an outsider to appreciate something like that to get us to see it through their eyes.

My parents went inside, leaving the two of us alone outside.

"So what do you think?" I asked her.

"Your parents are wonderful, and this city is beautiful," she replied, smiling at me. "Thank you for bringing me here."

I squeezed her hand, happy that she was enjoying herself. "So, I was thinking we could go in the hot tub tonight. How does that sound?"

If possible, her eyes lit up even more. "Your parents have a hot tub?"

"They sure do. Although they never use it. I'm sure they'll be grateful that it's finally going to be used. They also have a fireplace inside. Oh, and a firepit out here. So we could have a fire tonight too, if you wanted. Either inside or outside."

She smiled at me. "That all sounds heavenly. Do we have any plans for tomorrow?"

"Well, since you haven't been here yet, you definitely need to see Garden of the Gods. It's a must. We could either drive through it, or they have tons of hiking trails through it too. I was also thinking that it would be fun to take you to Manitou Springs. They have a ton of cute little shops, a huge outdoor arcade, and tons of hippies and wiccans."

"Sounds like our kind of town. Are your parents going to be upset if we go off to do our own thing while we're down here to visit them?"

"No, not at all. They will think it's a great idea for you to see all that while you're here. Plus, we're not in any sort of time crunch, so we can just do all that when we want and then come visit them before we head back home."

"Hey, for dinner, we were thinking Mexican. What do you girls think?" Mam asked, popping her head out.

"Ooh, Señor Manuel's?" I asked excitedly. It was one of our favorite restaurants in town. At Mam's nod, I smiled. "You like Mexican, right, babe?"

"Oh, fuck yes!" Anna exclaimed. She blushed before looking sheepishly at my mam. "Sorry Cara. I have the mouth of a sailor."

"Oh, dear, don't even worry about it."

"Yeah, my parents are even worse than you are. Especially her," I said, laughing at Mam's incredulous expression.

"Oh, that's not true at all," she protested before going inside.

"Should we go get ready for dinner?" I asked.

"Yes. Your girl is ready for a margarita. Where's my room at?" she asked.

"Your room? Don't you mean our room?"

A shocked expression crossed her beautiful face, making me laugh. "Your parents don't mind if we sleep together?"

"Siúcra, my parents don't have any problems with it. They know what grown couples do. Besides, I'm pretty sure my mam wants us to be living together already."

"Well, she is a smart lady," she teased with a twinkle in her eye. Was she saying what I thought she was?

"What do you mean by that?"

"That I wouldn't mind living with you," she said, seriously this time.

My jaw dropped. "Really?"

"Of course really. I love you. I know I've never lived with a significant other before, and that we've only been dating for like a month, but it feels right. There's no place I'd rather be than with you."

I felt tears welling up in my eyes. I had never lived with anyone either, but I wanted to so badly after that little speech. I kissed her with everything I was feeling for her, pulling back only when we were both thoroughly breathless.

"So we're going to live together?" I asked.

"Well, you have to say yes first," she teased, her smile lighting up her whole face.

"Yes," I told her, kissing her again. "On that note, let's go get ready to celebrate with my parents."

An hour and some dirty acts later, we were all piled into the car. Anna and I sat in the back seat quietly laughing our asses off as my da lectured my mam about her driving.

After we were seated at the restaurant and we had our drinks, I grabbed Anna's hand and looked at my folks. "So, we have news. Anna and I are moving in together."

Mam squealed excitedly. "Oh my goodness, I am so excited to hear that. You are by far my favorite of the girlfriends she's had."

"Mam," I admonished, shaking my head in embarrassment. While I was so glad she felt that way, I'm sure Anna didn't want to hear about Mam meeting my exes.

"Damn straight, I'm your favorite," Anna chirped next to me, raising her glass to clink my mam's.

"Oh, let's toast!" Mam exclaimed. We all raised our drinks to the middle of the table. Mam always had to give toasts. "To my beautiful daughter, and my beautiful *new* daughter. My baby couldn't have found a better woman for her."

We all clinked our glasses, and tears were gathering in Anna's eyes. I reached over and squeezed her hand. She looked over, giving me a slightly watery smile.

"So, are you moving in with her or is she moving in with you?" Da asked.

Both my and Anna's brows rose. We hadn't discussed that. "I'm not sure yet, Da. We literally just decided this right before coming to dinner."

"I bet it was because you met us, isn't that right, Anna dear?" Mam said, to which I rolled my eyes obnoxiously.

"Absolutely, Cara," Anna stated seriously, making Mam absolutely beam. When she looked away, Anna gave me a secret wink and a smile. I shook my head at the interaction, while inwardly dancing. I was thrilled that Anna liked my parents and that they all got along. I knew my family could be a bit crazy sometimes, and so could Anna. Maybe that's why they meshed well. I knew she would fit right in.

We continued chatting, drinking margaritas, and eating delicious food. I missed my parents. I didn't come down here often enough, and I promised myself then that I would make it a point to do so more frequently. Honestly, I missed this city too. I could totally see myself moving back here, but I wasn't sure if Anna would ever want to. Maybe I would make her fall in love with the city first, and then I would see if she would eventually be open to it. I knew there were plenty of acupuncture clinics around, including a community clinic. It was actually at that location that I decided that I wanted to do acupuncture for a living.

We finished up our dinner and headed back. The sun was just starting to descend by the time we walked in the door.

"Ready to test out the hot tub?" I asked.

"Oh hell yes."

I chuckled. "Okay, let's go get changed."

We did so quickly, with minimal touching, me in my olive green bikini, and Anna in her tight black one piece with strips of see-through material, and ten minutes later, we were sinking down into the gloriously hot water. Anna's enthusiastic moan had me blushing and clenching my thighs together. I turned the jets on and she got even more excited. I smiled to myself, thinking about how lucky I was to have found her. She opened her eyes to find me pretty much red as a tomato and squirming.

"Hear something you like?" she asked with a knowing smirk.

"Most definitely," I replied, crawling into her lap. Her hands made their way to my hips under the water. I leaned down, giving her a heated kiss, dragging my tongue along the seam of her lips. She whimpered against my mouth before opening hers, her tongue coming out to dance with mine.

Just as I started moving my hips against hers, I heard a hum and felt my hair flutter. Startled, I broke away, finding a hummingbird had just flown past us. My parents had multiple feeders set up outside, and Mam always had tons of hummers. Excited, I tapped Anna and pointed to where there were five gathered around one feeder.

"Oh my God. I love hummingbirds. I've never seen so many before!" she exclaimed. Indeed, the other feeder had six birds around it.

"They always are most active right before the sun sets," I told her. "They also know that my mam always has sugar water for them, so their house has become pretty popular over the years."

She watched in awe, her eyes darting between the two feeders for a long time before finally saying anything. "They're kind of little assholes to each other."

I laughed loudly. "Yes, they are. Hummingbirds are very territorial so they usually attack each other when they're at the feeders."

I was still watching her. I loved watching the birds, but honestly, the wonder on her face was the most beautiful thing I had ever seen, and I couldn't look away even if I wanted to. She finally noticed me staring.

"What?" she asked self-consciously. "Do I have something on my face?"

I smiled brightly at her. "Just wonder. That's all you have on your face. And it's the most gorgeous thing I've ever seen."

She blushed slightly, looking almost embarrassed, which was a little strange for Anna. I guess this was one of those rare moments when she let her true self shine through and she wasn't used to exposing herself like that.

"I've just never seen something like this. I mean I've seen hummingbirds before, obviously, but never like this. And those deer earlier. This place is amazing."

"It is. I miss it," I admitted.

She zeroed in on my face, studying me while looking like she was thinking intently. "Would you ever want to move back?" she asked, catching me off guard.

I looked around me, taking everything in. I did really miss living here, and I had just been thinking about bringing this up with her eventually. How soon did I want to though? Would that be too big of a change for her too soon?

"Yes," I answered honestly.

A big smile made its way across her face. "I think I would like living here."

I was so surprised that I just stared at her for about ten seconds. "Really? You would want to move here with me?"

"Of course. What's not to love? Your parents are here, it's a beautiful city, it's less crowded, not to mention cheaper."

"What about Savannah and Lauren?" I asked.

"What about them? I love them, but they both have their own lives now, their own relationships. And it's not like I'm never going to see them. They're only an hour and a half away."

"What about your job and apartment and my house?" I knew it sounded like I was trying to talk her out of it, but I just wanted her to think about everything before she made a decision.

"Babe, I love my apartment, but I'm sure we can find something that we both love here that would probably even be a better fit for us. I love your house too, but it's too small for both of us. And I'm sick of renting. I would like to own my own place. As for my job, it would be weird not working with Savannah anymore, but other than that, I wouldn't mind at all starting at a new shop. I like adventures," she finished simply.

Instead of replying verbally, I smiled as widely as my face would allow before bending down and taking her lips in a fierce kiss.

Chapter 18

Anna

The next day, we had breakfast with Molly's parents in our pajamas before getting ready for our adventures. Since I had never been to the Springs before, I was extremely excited. I had a feeling I was going to fall so in love with this town that I would never want to leave. We decided that we would hike through the Garden of the Gods instead of drive, before heading to Manitou.

I was in the middle of changing when I yawned and stretched. We had stayed up late the night before. Molly's parents went to bed early, so we camped out in the living room in front of the big fireplace. As we were cuddled up on the floor, Molly read *Harry Potter* out loud. Of course, it wasn't long before we were making love in front of the fire, and when we were done, we went back to reading. It was almost two a.m. before we made our way up to bed.

"Don't tempt me with these before we leave," Molly said, reaching around me from behind to wrap her hands around my tits as I had my arms stretched high.

"Hey, you're the one who kept me up so late last night, having your wicked way with me." I put my hands over hers and tilted my head to the side as she nuzzled my neck.

"Girls!" Cara yelled from downstairs, making me jump away from Molly guiltily. I still wasn't used to parents being okay with what we were doing under their roof.

Molly chuckled as she leaned in for a quick kiss. "I'll see what she wants. Put a shirt on and meet me downstairs."

I slapped her ass as she turned to leave, making her squeak slightly. When she was out the door, I turned back to my suitcase to finish getting dressed. I put on a little bit of makeup before heading down to the kitchen where everyone always seemed to gather.

"Mam is making us lunch so we can eat at the garden after our hike," Molly told me as I breezed in.

"Oh, thank you, Cara. That's very thoughtful of you."

She smiled at me. "Of course, dear. What would you like on your sandwich?"

When our lunches were packed and stocked with extra tomatoes from the garden, we headed out. Fifteen minutes later, we were pulling into the park, and I gasped, not even knowing where to look. There were huge red rock formations everywhere I glanced. Molly parked the car, grabbed the backpack with our food and water, and off we went. I stumbled a few times at first because I wasn't looking where I was walking.

"Why don't we just sit on this rock for a few minutes so you can take everything in, and not kill yourself before I have a chance to move in with you," Molly teased, chuckling as she led me somewhere I could sit down.

"I wouldn't kill myself. I'm coordinated enough where I would probably just end up paralyzed."

As I looked around, Molly started pointing out certain rock formations that she knew, the most famous one being the Kissing Camels. As soon as she mentioned it, all I could see was two camels kissing. When

I felt ready, we got up and took a nice leisurely hike, not going too quickly so I could admire anything new that we couldn't see before.

An hour and a half later, we were on higher ground and could see most of the park. We sat down and Molly got out our lunch and what was left of our water. As we sat there, she started telling me all the things she loved about the town, things she used to do here as a kid, places her parents took her when she was young. She painted such a wonderful picture in my head of this town, and her childhood, that it made me feel homesick for a town that I didn't know.

I wondered how my youth would've been if I hadn't been raised so religious, or if my mom was still around. I loved Molly's parents, but watching her with them made me ache for my mother, and my father if I was honest with myself. Despite everything that happened with him, I still loved him, and I wished things had turned out differently.

Molly also told me where the best places were to live in the city. We talked about different areas where we might want to start looking for houses. The more we talked, the more excited I got about this decision. It felt right, if a little quick and drastic, but let's be honest, that's how I operated. We discussed maybe having to live with her parents while we looked for a place, and that was totally fine with me. Plus we would both need to find jobs.

We finished up our lunch and headed back to the car. As much as I liked the garden, I was even more excited for Manitou. It sounded like my kind of place. I mean hippies and wiccans? What's not to love?

"We don't have time today, but maybe next time I'll take you to the Cave of the Winds. It's gorgeous there, and they do tours. It's very cool. They teach you all about the history, and tell you ghost stories."

"Ooh, that sounds like a blast."

Fifteen minutes later, we were pulling into the coolest town ever. The view was gorgeous, there were cute little shops everywhere, and everybody looked like they were walking on a cloud. Or just high.

Possibly both.

It took us a while to find a parking spot, and then we were out and about. Our first stop was of course to buy ice cream. I got butter pecan, and Molly got coffee flavor. We walked around town with our cones, making our way in and out of shops. My favorite shop we stopped in was called La Henna Boheme, and it was a straight up hippie shop, and they also did henna. Molly and I of course had them do us. I got my feet done and she got her hands.

After that, we stopped to get maté, and we took it with us as we made our way through the penny arcade. Molly pointed out all of the rides they had when she was little, even getting on one that she barely fit in. We played games until we ran out of change.

We also stumbled across an old photo booth that printed off pictures in black and white. We of course took full advantage, making the most ridiculous faces we could and made out for the last one (big surprise there). Molly also made me drink the water from the springs. They had little fountains all throughout the town that connected directly to the spring. She hadn't told me they were naturally carbonated, and at the first taste I almost spit it out immediately. Once I knew what to expect, it wasn't as bad. She also told me that the waters were said to have healing qualities to them.

We walked hand in hand almost the entire trip, and did not get one judgmental look. That right there made it all the more sweet and made me fall in love with the town even more.

"So what did you think?" Molly asked when we got back to her car.

"Can we live here?"

"You loved it that much?" she asked, laughing.

"I did. It's like we were meant to be here."

"I'm glad you loved it." She smiled at me and squeezed my hand.

We drove back to Molly's parents' house. We had a quick dinner with them before packing up and heading back home. As we left I had tears in my eyes from the hug that Cara had given me. She also whispered in my ear that she knew I was the right one for her daughter, making me feel wonderful. I finally felt like I was a part of a family again, and I was so thankful that they welcomed me so readily.

"Your house or mine?" Molly asked as we neared Denver.

"Mine. I want to watch *Gone with the Wind* tonight," I told her as she nodded in reply. "So, do you think you'll sell your place, or rent it out?"

"I'll sell. It's an old house, and I don't want to deal with any repairs. Plus we'll be far enough away that I don't want to hire someone to deal with it, but I also don't want to drive down here every time something needs to be dealt with."

"That makes sense. When do we want to do this? I'm excited to start looking at houses. Oooh, we should start a Zillow search when we get home!" I exclaimed. I knew I was being a little intense, but I was stoked, and I could tell Molly didn't mind in the slightest by the big smile on her face.

"I mean, we can start the whole process as soon as you'd like. We'll obviously need to put notice in at work, and I'm not sure how long the whole house selling process will take, but I'm guessing that will be at least a month to two months. Maybe we should plan for like three months?"

"That sounds perfect. That'll give me plenty of time with the girls too. I will miss them," I said, getting slightly emotional. I knew we were making the right choice, but they were like my family.

Molly reached over and squeezed my hand. "I know you will, siúcra. They'll miss you too." I nodded, swallowing past the lump in my throat.

Ten minutes later we were pulling up to my apartment. We brought our stuff in, and from all the travel and the big day that we had, I immediately wanted to take a shower. I heard Molly enter the bathroom as soon as I stepped under the spray, and felt her behind me not long after.

"Want me to wash your hair?" she whispered in my ear.

A nod was my only reply. I turned to wet my scalp as she filled her hands with shampoo, and then her fingers were in my hair, her strong hands massaging away any tension. I moaned out loud, not even trying to stop myself. She was very thorough, even getting along the back where the neck and head meet.

"Rinse," she said, her voice rough with need.

I did as I was bid, and as soon as I was done, she repeated the process with conditioner. Then, after I rinsed that out, she lathered my body with my lavender-scented body wash on a loofah. The caresses were slowly driving me mad. Even though I used the loofah every time I showered, it felt monumentally different in her hands. She alternated between long, gentle strokes and slow circles. Every time she came up on an interesting area, she would skirt around it, washing and touching everywhere except where I wanted her most.

"Molly, please," I pleaded when I couldn't take it anymore.

"I love when you beg me," she whispered against my mouth before plunging her tongue between my lips. She finally gave me what I wanted and dragged the loofah between my legs. I made all the encouraging noises I could, but soon I wanted more. I spun her around, pushed her against the shower wall, and rubbed my body against hers. With all the soap covering my torso, she felt slippery against me and it added a whole new sensation. I sucked her lip into my mouth and bit down slightly, before pulling back and trailing my mouth down her body, making little nips in all the right places as I went.

When I was kneeling in front of her, I lifted her foot and set it on the side of the tub, opening her up to me. I licked up her seam before switching methods as I slowly dragged my nipple piercing along the same path. With each pass along her clit, pleasure shot from my chest down to my drenched cunt. Soon she was thrusting against my breast all on her own, and at the sight, I couldn't take it anymore and reached down to touch myself. Her eyes latched on to mine as her own hands went to her nipples. Minutes later, we were both panting and straining as we rushed toward the edge.

"Come for me, Molly," I bit out, not able to hold back anymore.

With a cry she came against my tit, and I finally let go, groaning against her stomach. We stayed there for God knows how long as we both caught our breath. Finally, when I didn't feel like I would fall flat on my face, I stood up, giving her a heated kiss before I turned us toward the spray to rinse off the body wash.

When we were all dried off and in our comfy clothes, we finally made our way into bed, and turned on *Gone with the Wind*. We snuggled up next to each other, and we were both asleep within five minutes.

Chapter 19

Molly

The next week passed in a blur. I found a Realtor, and started the process of getting my house on the market. It involved a lot of cleaning, fixing random things, and packing up all the shit that wasn't essential. Anna helped me whenever we were off together, but it was a lot of work.

We hadn't told the girls yet, but we were planning on telling them when we went out that weekend for our couples' night.

There was one big thing I did want to do before we moved, and that was to have Savannah tattoo me. I knew she could still do that after we moved, but I didn't want to have to drive all that way if I could get it done beforehand.

Luckily, I had my tattoos scheduled two days before our couples' night, and I was so excited.

"You're working tomorrow, right?" I asked Anna the night before.

"Yes, I am. And I already checked, and I don't have any appointments scheduled at the time you're supposed to come in."

I nodded in reply. As excited as I was, I was still very nervous. I didn't have many tattoos, and I was also going to someone new. I just wanted it to turn out exactly as I pictured in my head, and I hoped that Savannah would be able to deliver.

"Hey," Anna gently said, catching my attention. "Savannah is great. You don't need to be nervous, okay?"

I smiled at her this time, squeezing her hand in thanks. She was right. I knew Savannah was good, otherwise Anna would never let me get tattooed by her.

"It sounds like you need a distraction," she purred in my ear as she slid the strap of my tank top off my shoulder, her lips following the same path. She then proceeded to thoroughly distract me.

The next morning, I woke up early. Too filled with nervous, excited energy to sleep anymore. I took a shower, making sure to get the spots I was getting tattooed extra clean, then made some tea, leaving extra hot water in the teakettle for Anna, and then I made us breakfast. I was too nervous to eat much, but I knew Anna always appreciated when I did this for her and it kept me busy.

Anna came out just as I was taking the eggs off the stove and buttering the toast. I set it in front of her before getting her some tea. When I set her mug down, she was already halfway through her breakfast. I chuckled as I took a bite out of my own toast before washing it down with a gulp of tea.

"What did I do in my past life to deserve you?" Anna moaned as she shoveled food into her mouth. I knew she was halfway joking, but I still brightened at the praise.

"Something pretty great since I'm so awesome," I replied like a smart-ass. *Anna must be rubbing off on me,* I thought.

"I was probably a nun or something. I bet I helped a lot of orphans." I laughed loudly at that. Anna was the very last person I could picture as a nun. "So, are you excited? Your tattoo is in just a couple short hours."

"Yes. I'm very excited. I just hope it turns out how I want it."

"Stop worrying. It'll turn out even better than you're picturing.

Believe me. I've worked next to Savannah for years and that's always the first thing out of people's mouths."

I felt a rush of relief at her words, and my excitement doubled.

We relaxed with each other for the rest of the morning, chatting, drinking tea, and just generally touching each other. Finally, hours later, it was time for us to start getting ready and to head into the shop.

As we pulled up, Anna pointed out Savannah's car in the parking lot, which I was happy about since it meant we could start early.

"Hey girl hey!" Savannah exclaimed as we walked in, and I could tell she was almost as excited as I was. "Are you ready? I already have a printout for your approval." She handed it over immediately and my nerves went right out the door. Anna was right. It was even better than I imagined.

"Oh, Savannah. It's perfect. Just what I was wanting." She smiled at the praise and went to print off the stencil.

"Told ya," Anna whispered in my ear before smacking my ass. "I need to go set up my station, but I'll be there when she starts, okay?"

I nodded and quickly went to the bathroom before we got started.

When I came back out, Savannah called me over to her station, which was already mostly set up from the looks of it. She shaved my right inner forearm, and the spot behind my left ear, and wiped off both spots with solution. She then took the stencils she had printed off and took her time placing both of them. When she had done that she had me check the mirror to make sure I liked the placement. They both looked perfect, and I told her that.

We decided to do the big one first, so Savannah had me sit on a chair on the opposite side of the table from her with my forearm laid out in front of me. My nerves came back just the slightest as I saw her get the needle out and the gun ready. I took a few deep breaths and suddenly felt Anna behind me, her hands massaging my shoulders. I relaxed slightly, and then it was time to get started.

"Ready?" At my nod, she started in. Within minutes, I was settling back into my chair. The pain wasn't bad, and I knew she was going to do a great job.

"You forgot to turn on the music, bitch. I should do that before the guys get in and put on something stupid," Anna pointed out. "Any requests, ladies?"

"How about Flogging Molly?" I asked. It seemed fitting since I was getting an Ireland tattoo. Plus I loved them. And any Irish music, to be honest.

As the music started up, I relaxed even more, smiling. "Good choice, my love," Anna said, sitting down next to me this time. "So, did everybody find their outfits for Friday yet?"

"Yes, we all did. I don't know what Lauren's and Nix's are going to be, but Lauren seemed pretty excited."

"You know what I was thinking would also be fun, not to mention even more absurd?" Anna asked. "What if we had our significant others also do our makeup?"

Before I could even process what that would mean, Savannah busted out laughing so hard I thought she was going to fuck up a line. "Oh God. We are going to look absolutely awful. I mean if we're going to do it, let's go all the way. I'm down. Can you text Lauren?"

Before she even asked, Anna had her phone out and was furiously typing away. Moments later we heard her phone ding with a message.

"She says, and I quote, 'Nix is going to kill you.' So I think that means she's down too."

Already thoughts were coming into my head of how I was going to do Anna's makeup.

"What do you think? Are we going ridiculous on each other, or beautiful makeup?" I asked her.

"Hey, that's no fair! You have to do your makeup like drag queens too, otherwise Lauren and I are going to look even more horrible,"

Savannah complained.

"She does bring up a fantastic point," Anna added with a mischievous glint to her eye, no doubt already scheming.

"So, on a separate note, have you guys started trying yet?" Anna asked Savannah.

"Not quite yet. I get my IUD taken out next week. The doctor told me I can get pregnant as soon as it's out, but I'm guessing I'm going to have some hormonal adjustments before my body is back to normal. I mean, I've been on birth control for over ten years now."

"Yeah, that makes sense. I hate birth control. I'm so glad I don't have to worry about it anymore. It made me crazy."

"I'm so thankful I've never had to be on it," I added. They both turned stunned gazes to me. "What? I'm a lesbian, remember?"

They both nodded then proceeded to tell me how jealous they were that I never had to experience the awfulness.

"How's Charlie feeling about all of it?"

"He's, you know, a typical guy. Excited, but scared shitless. I mean, I am too. It's terrifying thinking about being responsible for another little life, but I feel so ready for it. I mean, until I call you, freaking the fuck out about the fact that I'm pregnant," she joked.

We continued chatting while Savannah worked. It was really cool to be able to see the piece come together. With my chest piece I didn't have that luxury. About halfway through, Anna got a walk-in. She went to her station, professional as can be. Well, professional for Anna.

"So, how's it going with you guys?" Savannah asked since we were finally alone.

"It's going really great," I told her as I looked at Anna. She gave me a knowing smile and a wink, causing me to blush.

"You really love her, don't you?" Savannah asked.

"Yes. I really do," I told her with all sincerity.

"Good," she said, smiling, before turning very serious and a little scary. "Because that beautiful woman has been through so much. She deserves all the happiness in the world. So I like you, but if you fuck her over, you'll have to answer to me and Lauren. Got it?"

"Savannah, I'm so grateful that she has friends like you who have her back. I would never hurt her in a million years. She's who I've been looking for my whole life."

She smiled widely at me again before returning to my arm.

"How's it going over here, ladies?" Anna asked about ten minutes later.

"Great," Savannah said. "We're almost done with this one and then I'll quickly do her needle."

Twenty minutes later, I was looking in the mirror at both my tattoos. I couldn't believe how perfect they were. I didn't care that Savannah was going to be an hour and a half away after we moved, I was going to keep going to her.

I rushed over to her and gave her a big hug, taking her slightly by surprise. "Thank you. I love them so much." She gave me a quick squeeze before pulling away to wrap them for me. I quickly paid, giving her a very generous tip, especially since I knew she gave me a good deal, before heading over to Anna.

"What do you think?" I asked.

"I love them," she told me excitedly. "She did such a wonderful job."

"I'm glad you like them. And you were right. They are even better than I pictured."

"Oh stop," Savannah said with a wave of her hand. "You guys are giving me a big head."

"Savannah, that should be your slogan. 'This tattoo will be even better than you could've possibly imagined,'" Anna teased.

Savannah flipped her off, lovingly of course, before returning to cleaning her station.

"Want me to clean those for you later?" Anna purred.

"Oh God, please say yes," one of the guys said.

"And then go into explicit details about how you want her to do it," another chimed in.

I rolled my eyes obnoxiously before leaning in to give Anna a quick kiss goodbye. She, of course, deepened it. Not able to help myself, I returned with equal fervor. We broke apart as soon as we heard the guys groaning. As you can imagine, a tremendous blush rose to my cheeks.

"Don't pay attention to them," Anna whispered. "See you at home, hot stuff."

With that I headed home. Completely content.

Chapter 20

Anna

Two days later, it was the day of the big triple date. I was bouncing around with excitement because the six of us had never hung out together before. I knew that Savannah and Lauren were really looking forward to it too. At four o'clock, Molly and I started getting ready. We put on our hideous dresses, found shoes that sort of matched, and then started on hair and makeup. We left the hair pretty simple since the outfits and most likely the makeup were going to be so drastic and ridiculous.

Molly did a little pinned bump with her bangs in the front, curling the rest in loose waves. I just did a braid from my left side that wrapped around the back and kept the hair on my right side down.

It was time for makeup, and I was planning on being super obnoxious with Molly's. I mean, have you met me? I had her sit down, and I put on foundation first. Then I put on a shit ton of blush (not that she needed it anyway), followed by a highlighter, which I put on her cheeks, the tip of her nose, and her collarbones. For eyeshadow, I went with the most vibrant color in my makeup box, a bright mermaid blue, and I topped it with gold glitter. I gave her a cat eyeliner and put some fake eyelashes on her. I finished her look with a horrid orange lipstick that I didn't even know I had.

She looked in the mirror. "Well, what do you think?" I asked.

"God I hate you sometimes. Also, I'm glad you did me first so I can make yours just as terrible." I grinned broadly at the praise.

"Bring it on, baby."

Twenty minutes later, my own makeup was done. Pink. Everywhere. Not a subtle pink either, bright fucking bubblegum pink. Blush, eyeshadow, lips, you name it. I also had on the biggest fake lashes known to mankind. I laughed loudly as I looked at both of us in the mirror. We looked absolutely horrifying. I couldn't wait for the public to see us in all of our glory. I could only imagine how our counterparts would fare.

Our first location was on South Pearl Street, and since my apartment was closest, we decided to all meet up there and Uber over together. Molly and I had a glass of wine while we waited for everyone to arrive. It was good for us to do, because for some inexplicable reason, I was fairly anxious. I chalked it up to going to such a crowded event when I'd had a panic attack in public not too long prior.

At five thirty, everybody showed up, and as I opened the door, I almost choked on my wine. We were definitely going to give the public quite a shock.

Savannah was in what looked like the ugliest prom dress I had ever seen. It was aquamarine, almost teal, and strapless with a sweetheart neckline. It was a ball gown style and the fitted top half had tons of fake jewels glued to it. The color clashed tremendously with her red hair and somehow her yellow eyeshadow also clashed with everything, making it ten times worse. Her makeup looked decently done (I mean, for a man), but the colors were all wrong.

Her counterpart, Charlie, was wearing a pair of cat shorts with a white button-down shirt and matching cat vest. The shorts and the vest just had pictures of cat faces on them and I couldn't believe they found a set. His look was complete with a black bow tie and a matching fedora. It looked like Savannah also took the liberty of doing his hair in a pair of pigtail braids.

Lauren was wearing a long-sleeve, multicolored, diamond-patterned sequined top that looked like it was from the eighties, shoulder pads and all. She also had on a floor-length pleated black skirt, and her makeup was godawful. Nix had not done a good job. She had fuchsia eyeshadow, and her eyeliner was very thick and slightly crooked. Her mascara was clumpy and I was pretty sure I saw a small blotch of it on one eyelid. Her blush looked like it had been painted on, and he had topped off the look with bright red lipstick. Her partner in crime, Nix, was wearing tight-ass leather pants that left very little to the imagination, a dragon button-up shirt, and the best part, a Macklemore-style jacket. It was tiger-striped with so much fake fur on the collar that it almost swallowed him whole. She had also given him a pompadour hair style and made him wear white-framed sunglasses.

"Well, I think we're going to give the people of Denver quite a show," I said.

"Understatement of the year," Nix grumbled.

"I already called for an Uber," Lauren stated, undeterred by Phoenix's enthusiasm. "It's right around the corner so we should head down."

Fifteen minutes later, we were at our destination, Sushi Den. We decided to eat first and then walk around after. We had already gotten many strange looks from people, particularly our driver, and I obnoxiously smiled and waved in response to each one.

We were quickly sat since we had a reservation, and we all ordered drinks to top off the fun of the night. We marked up the sushi page with more food than I had ever ordered in my life, also ordering three appetizers. After our drinks came and we had our order in, I looked at Molly and squeezed her hand.

"You guys, we have news," I told everyone.

"Well, don't keep us in suspense. What is it?" Savannah asked.

"We're moving in together."

The girls exclaimed excitedly, as I knew they would. The guys of course were polite and probably didn't give a shit, but nevertheless they still offered congratulations with smiles on their faces.

"That's not all. We're moving to Colorado Springs."

Silence greeted us for several moments. Molly put her hand on my back in support. I'm sure she could feel my anxiety.

"Well, that's exciting!" Lauren finally blurted.

"We're going to miss your stupid face around here though," Savannah interjected sullenly.

"I know. And I will miss you bitches too. But we will only be an hour and a half away. It's not like you'll never see me. Plus we can finally all go on our Ireland trip together."

"Oh, that's true!" Conversation quickly turned to said trip, for which I was very grateful. Molly chipped in with all of her Irish knowledge, and we soon had a rough plan in place. Within six months we were going to try to go. Who knew that the picture I had in my head of being tangled up in the bedsheets of a castle with the beautiful redhead beside me would actually come true?

Halfway through dinner, a shiver made its way up my spine, but I shrugged it off. I wasn't going to let anything ruin my night with my favorite people in the world.

Our waitress came up to the table and we ordered another round of drinks, but as we did so, I had an idea. "So, we have a little contest going on here. Will you do us a favor and bring a shot of your choice to the person who you think has the ugliest outfit?" I asked our waitress. She laughed before nodding and heading on her way.

"Who do you think it will be?" Molly asked.

"I have no clue. I mean, we're all pretty hideous," Lauren said.

Minutes later, she had our round of drinks on a tray. We all sat there tense as she passed them around, wanting to see who would get the shot. Finally, she set a shot in front of Nix, and I busted out laughing when I realized she brought him a "blow job" shot. I immediately took my phone out to film. This was something I never thought I would witness.

"Are you fuckin' kidding me?" He sulked, making us all laugh even harder.

"Come on, babe. Wrap your lips around it and tip it back," Lauren encouraged, a naughty gleam in her eyes. "I know that wicked mouth is strong enough for it."

"You're in for a spanking later," I heard him whisper.

"Will you wear those pants when you do it?" she asked with heated eyes. He rolled his before bending down and taking the shot like a champ. We all cheered, including the waitress, when he was done.

"For the record, I hate you all," he concluded in typical Nix fashion, even though he had a big smile on his face.

We all finished eating, and I mean, we ate *all* of it. We decided to get some tempura cheesecake, each couple with their own. When dinner was finally over, we took to the streets.

I had never been to a First Friday before, but I was stoked to see what the night had in store. Our first stop was at a gallery that had tons of pottery and fine jewelry. As we browsed, I decided to buy some nice jewelry for Molly before the night was through. There were lots of pieces she stopped to look at and that fit her complexion.

When that spot was tapped out, we went to a place that one of the potters recommended. It was called Colorado Potters Guild, and you could watch while the artists turned pieces on the wheel. It was crazy watching them turn a lump of clay into something so beautiful. It took shape with the slightest of their movements, and before you knew it, you had a completed pot.

Lauren had taken pottery in high school, and she was telling us a little bit about what they were doing. She also went into all the stuff that was super difficult that, of course, the artists made look easy, like centering the clay.

We watched them for God knows how long, but then we finally felt ready to leave.

"So, what do you guys want to see next?" I asked as we walked out.

"Well, I've heard Bell Studio is pretty cool to see, which isn't far," Charlie suggested. "They have oil paintings, more pottery I think, and stained glass."

"Oh wait," Savannah said, stopping us. "Before we go, I want someone to take a picture of us all."

The group of girls behind us heard her, and volunteered to take the photo. We took a few, some nice ones, and of course some funny ones. We thanked them and were on our way to the next shop when it happened.

It was a rare moment when there was hardly anyone around us; we were enjoying it, taking up space and laughing among ourselves, when a tall, homeless looking man, with dark hair and lots of tattoos stopped directly in front of our group. The shivers returned to my spine, and my stomach sank like a rock. I just knew that something terrible was about to happen.

"Greg," Savannah whispered, her fingers clutching tightly to her purse. "You're not supposed to be here," she said more forcefully.

"Why not? 'Cause you say so? You fucked up my life, you cunt!" he roared, spittle flying from his mouth. Before I could register what was happening, he leveled a gun right at Savannah's chest. Without thinking, I threw myself in front of her. I heard a shot fire, someone screaming, and then everything went black.

Chapter 21

Anna

Everything was dark. That was all I was aware of at first. I kept trying to open my eyes to see what was going on around me, but my eyelids wouldn't move. I focused on my other senses, but I wasn't getting anything from them either. I was stuck.

Had I died? If so, shouldn't I be seeing a light I was supposed to walk toward? Maybe I was in limbo. Or purgatory. That was a thing, right? Oh yeah, it was, 'cause at that moment, I remembered the most random scene from a wonderfully terrible movie. In The Haunting*, the main chick, who is possibly the worst actress in the world, is telling Catherine Zeta-Jones that she was stuck in purgatory for eleven years. I laughed at the time, but at the moment, all I could think was that I really hoped that didn't end up happening to me.*

Minutes passed. Or maybe hours. Days? I had no clue. I had a hard time remembering what had happened. Why was I here? No matter how hard I thought, I couldn't remember for the life of me. Wouldn't that be great, dying but having no idea how? I guess it would depend on the way I died. If it was horrific, I wouldn't want to remember something like that.

Oh God. I was rambling even in my own thoughts. I guess that's what happened when you had absolutely nothing to distract you except your own brain. I also felt like I was forgetting someone very important. Now that I thought about it, the details of my life seemed fuzzy. Like a radio station I couldn't tune into. It was on the tip of my mind but I just couldn't grasp it.

After an undetermined amount of time in "The Nothing," as I liked to call it, I finally started to sense something. No, not something. Someone. The shape was directly in front of me. Blurry at first, then slowly coming into focus. When she finally emerged, a sob caught in my throat.

"Mom," I breathed.

"Hi, my Hannah Banana," she said, smiling, tears running down her beautiful face.

"How are you here? Am I dead? For real?" I asked, terrified now. I had joked about the possibility in my own head, but I couldn't fathom actually being dead. And leaving Molly. Oh God. Molly. It was the first time I had thought of her in this place. Finally a piece of myself that had come back to me. She must be going crazy with worry or grief.

"No, darling. It's not your time yet. You have a special lady waiting for you."

"Mom. It's really you?" I asked, not daring to believe this was real.

"Yes, honey. It's really me."

I didn't think twice. I hurled myself into her arms, burying my face in her neck. She smelled just like I remembered, brown sugar and cinnamon, and tears streamed down my face. I could scarcely breathe from sobbing so hard.

"Mama. I've missed you so much." Her arms tightened around me at the confession.

"I've missed you too. I want you to know that I'm so proud of you. You're such an amazing woman, and I've loved watching you grow into the beautiful, strong woman you've become."

I clung to her words as well as her body, soaking up the assurance I didn't know I needed.

"Why are you here?" I asked, reluctantly letting her go so I could look into

her face.

"To help you remember so you can make your way back," she stated as if it was the simplest thing in the world. "You still have a lot left to do in your life, sweet girl."

"I don't want to leave you yet," I admitted.

"We have a little bit of time," she said, clearly not wanting to part with me either.

"So, what's the afterlife like?" I asked, curious despite myself.

"You know I can't tell you that," she said, a gleam in her eye.

"Are you happy? Can you at least tell me that? Meet any hot guys up in heaven?" I teased.

Her laugh rang out like a bell. God, how I'd missed that sound. "I am happy, darling. What about you? Does that nice woman you're with make you happy?" It was the second time she had mentioned Molly. The old part of me shrank away at her knowing, hoping she wouldn't judge me for it.

"Yes. She makes me happier than anyone I've ever met. She's my other half."

"That's all that matters to me," my mother said gently, stroking my cheek softly with her thumb. A light burst inside of me, and I felt some broken part of me that had been there for a long time start to mend. "It's almost time, sweetie. But before you go, one more thing. Forgive your father."

I froze at the words.

"I know what happened," she said softly, tears gathering in her eyes. "He's a changed man. Trust me." Before I could reply she started to fade right before my eyes. "I love you, Hannah Banana."

"I love you too, Mama." And then she was gone and the blackness returned.

Chapter 21

The first sense that returned was touch. I could feel myself lying in a soft bed, with somewhat scratchy sheets covering me. I could also feel a warm, soft hand wrapped in mine. I tried to squeeze it, but apparently I couldn't move yet. The worst thing I felt, though, was a sharp, throbbing pain in my chest. Sometimes it was slightly dull, sometimes it was more intense, radiating pain through my back and down my arms.

The next sense that returned was sound. At first all I could hear was beeping. A heart rate monitor, I realized. After some time, I started hearing voices. It took me a while to discern who they were and what they were saying.

"Why hasn't she woken up yet?" Molly asked. I could hear the stress and worry coating her voice. I wished I could do something to comfort her. I doubled my efforts, tried to open my eyes or move my hand, even a finger, but my body refused to cooperate.

"Her body is recovering. All of her vitals look good, she just needs time to rest. She'll come around when she's ready," an unfamiliar voice replied before the door opened and shut. Molly sighed and laid her head on our joined hands.

"Siúcra, I miss you so much. I wish you would open those beautiful blue eyes for me." I could hear that she was on the verge of crying, and it broke my heart. "You know, there was a male nurse who came in here and was checking me out," she teased with a conspiratorial note in her voice. "You need to wake up so you can yell at him for me and stake your claim."

I inwardly smiled to myself, promising to do just that when I woke up, before the blackness returned.

When I came around this time, I could already tell more senses had returned. I could smell the antiseptic scent that filled every hospital, but that never fully covered the smell of sickness and death. I also caught a hint of shitty hospital food.

"God, I wish she would wake up," I heard a new voice say. Lauren.

"Me too. I hate this. I don't know how you can stand it, Molly," another voice added. Savannah. Sweet relief poured through me when I heard her voice, but I couldn't remember why I felt that way.

"I'm about to crawl out of my skin," Molly replied tiredly.

"I can't believe she's been out for a week and they have no idea when she's going to wake up," Lauren said. Jesus. It had been a whole week? I bet Molly was going out of her mind.

I heard one of the girls walk over to my bedside. "Bitch, if you can hear me, get the fuck up. We miss you and we're worried about you," Savannah scolded.

"And when you do wake up, we are going to cunt-punt you across the room. You hear me?" Lauren chimed in from across the room. With all of their *encouragement* I tried as hard as I could to do anything. Literally anything at all. Nothing.

So. Frustrating.

"We're all here waiting for you when you wake up, my love," Molly said, as if she could tell how frustrated I was, giving me a kiss on the head.

Blackness returned.

The first thing I noticed this time was Molly reading me *Harry Potter.* I instantly relaxed at the sound of her voice reading one of my favorite books. When she finished the chapter, I heard her close the book and set it down.

"Maybe I can get you to wake up by telling you some terrible HP pick-up lines. 'You may be a muggle, but that body is magical,'" she whispered in my ear. I felt myself huff out the tiniest bit of air out of my nose as I tried to laugh. Molly paused and seemed to be still as a statue. "Okay, let's try another one," she said hopefully. "How about 'Did you survive the Avada Kedavra curse? Because you are drop dead gorgeous.'

"I'd let you Slytherin," I croaked out.

"Oh Anna. Thank God!" Molly exclaimed as I opened my eyes. "Let me get the doctor." She burst through the door and ran down the hall before I knew what was happening. Probably only thirty seconds later she returned with the doctor on her heels. She was immediately back at my side, the doctor at my other.

"What happened?" I whispered. My throat felt so dry. She quickly picked up a glass of water and held a straw in front of me. I drank greedily before the doctor reminded me to drink slowly.

"What do you remember?" Molly asked.

I racked my brain but everything felt so fuzzy. "I remember going on our triple date. I remember Nix doing the blow job shot. I vaguely remember watching the potters on the wheels."

"Well, after that, we were walking down the street to go to our next stop, and Greg showed up. He leveled a gun at Savannah and you jumped in front of her. The bullet hit you in the chest, but luckily did not get your heart or any major arteries. But you lost a lot of blood."

Now that she mentioned it, I could feel the spot in my chest where I had been hit. At the moment, it just felt like a dull, manageable pain. My mind was reeling. "What happened to Greg? Is Savannah okay?"

"She's fine. You gave her enough time to pull her own gun. Greg's dead." I breathed a huge sigh of relief, which was slightly uncomfortable. I had never been more grateful to my past self for making sure she got her concealed carry.

"How long have I been out?"

"A week and a half. I've been going out of my mind."

I gave her a hand a squeeze.

"I'm so sorry, Molly. I hate that I made you feel that way.

"Anna, stop. It's okay. I'm just glad you're all right and that you're finally here with me." She gave me a gentle kiss on the lips, which I tried to deepen, but she pulled away before I could injure myself.

The doctor proceeded to ask me a few questions and told me I would need to stay a few more days in the hospital, but that everything looked good and I was healing well.

Molly texted the girls, and I was sure they were rushing over as fast as they could. Sure enough, ten minutes later, they burst through the door.

"Oh, Anna. I'm so glad you're okay," Lauren said, looking like she was about to hug me, but then thought better of it.

"I can't believe you did that for me," Savannah told me. There were tears in her eyes as she came up and gently kissed my cheek. "You almost died to save me. I don't know whether to punch you, or buy you everything you ever want."

I laughed, but quickly stopped at the discomfort. "Well, how about you start with the second, and then I'll let you punch me once I'm fully healed. Deal?"

"Only as long as you never do anything like that again," she compromised.

"Well, I would, but I'm planning on getting shot again next week."

"Smart ass," all three of them muttered. I lovingly gave them the finger.

A nurse walked in and I told her I needed to use the restroom. She had everyone leave before she took out my catheter and, as embarrassing as it was, helped me do my business and brush my teeth before going back to bed. Someone had changed the sheets while we were busy, and it felt glorious to lie back down in them.

When I was all settled, Molly came back in. I was already half asleep. "Where are the girls?" I yawned.

"They knew you were going to be tired so they left. They're going to come back tomorrow."

I nodded. As much as I loved them, I was grateful I wouldn't have to socialize. I didn't have the energy.

"Sleep, siúcra. I'll be here when you wake up.

"Come up here with me," I requested, holding out my hand in invitation.

"Anna, as much as I want to, I don't know if I should." Molly worried her bottom lip between her teeth.

"Please?" I asked, getting slightly teary. After everything that happened, I just needed to feel her close to me.

"Oh, baby, don't cry. I'll come in with you." I scooted over to make room for her, and as soon as she lay down, she opened her arms to me. I immediately cuddled up to her, soaking in the feel of her arms around me and the pounding of her heart beneath my ear. I was asleep seconds later.

Two days later, I was finally starting to feel quite a bit better. I could get up and go to the bathroom on my own. I still wasn't able to shower by myself, but Molly helped me take a bath the day before. The girls had been by multiple times, and I was grateful to see them each day.

Savannah kept her word and kept continually bringing me things. Food, flowers, chocolate, good-smelling shower stuff, you name it, she brought it.

We were all hanging out, playing rummy and eating the sweets that Savannah had brought that day, when Karen, my favorite nurse, walked in.

"Anna, you have another visitor." I looked around, confused. Everyone that I would expect to come and see me was here.

"Who is it?" I asked.

"It's your father," she stated simply, smiling because she had no idea what those words did to me. My stomach bottomed out, and I quickly got up and made it to the toilet just in time to throw up everything I had eaten that day.

Molly came in behind me and held my hair back. Embarrassment flooded me at her seeing me like this. When I was done, she grabbed a glass of water for me. I swished out my mouth before tentatively taking a few drinks. When I was sure I was done getting sick, I flushed the toilet and brushed my teeth, eventually making my way back into my room.

"Do you want me to tell him to leave?" Karen asked me gently.

I almost said yes, but something stopped me. Something in the corner of my brain that I couldn't quite grasp. "No. Send him in," I said, surprising everyone in the room from the looks of it.

When Karen left, Molly put her hand on my back. "Are you sure, Anna? You've been through a lot. No one would think less of you if you decided not to see him."

"I'm sure. It's time."

"Do you want us to stay or go?" Lauren asked.

"I'm not sure yet," I answered truthfully. "Stay for now."

I sat on the bed, and Molly stood behind me, keeping her hand on my back in support. A moment later, my father walked in. I inhaled sharply. It was my dad. He was gray and slightly wrinkled, but it was my dad. His eyes were much warmer than I'd ever seen them, and at the moment they were also full of relief, fear, and concern.

"Hannah Banana," he said, his voice rough. I felt tears building behind my eyes, but I blinked them back.

"Hi, Dad."

"Honey, I am so sorry." I closed my eyes at the words. Words I'd been wanting to hear for over ten years. I struggled to hold myself together. "I know that doesn't mean much after all this time, but I've been wanting to say that to you for so long. I've been looking for you ever since you left."

"How did you find me?" I asked when I finally felt like I could speak without sobbing.

"The news. We heard about the shooting and saw a video of you being put in the ambulance."

My heart stopped. "Who's we?" I asked.

"Me, your stepmother, and Nathan. We're all here, but I thought I should come to see you alone first."

"Nathan?" I asked, horrified. "How could you bring him here? He's who I was running away from."

"I know. He knows that too. He told me everything after you left. You don't have to see him if you don't want to, but I need to tell you that he's a changed man. He was a young boy with lots of mental issues when you two met, and since then, he's gotten a lot of therapy and worked through those issues. He knows you might never forgive him, and he's okay with that, but he wanted me to tell you how deeply sorry he is."

I took a deep breath, and I felt the tears finally falling down my face as I looked at my father. I didn't know what to think or what to say. My whole world had been flipped on its head. Molly rubbed my back in slow circles, and the girls looked at me with concerned and hopeful gazes.

"Can you ladies leave us, please?" I asked. I finally felt brave enough to face him on my own. One by one they all got up and walked to the door.

"I'll be right outside if you need me, siúcra," Molly said softly as she closed the door behind her.

"How could you do it?" I asked him, tears coming stronger now. "You were supposed to be the one person to have my back. The one person to take on the world for me. Mom was gone. It was just you, and instead of believing your own *fucking* daughter," I seethed, not caring that I was swearing and yelling at him, "you disregarded me completely, making me feel like I was being a disobedient child for something that *was done to me*!" I shouted, unable to control myself.

I was breathing heavily and I could feel my heart rate getting dangerously high. I closed my eyes, counted to ten, and continued to take deep, calming breaths. When I opened my eyes, my father had tears running down his own cheeks, and the sight broke my heart.

"I can give you all the excuses in the world, that I thought you were acting out because your mother had died, that you didn't like that I had remarried, that you wanted my attention, but what it all really boiled down to was my own selfish greed and need for power. All I could see was that this incident was going to get in my way of finally getting what I wanted. That I would finally be in a position of power with the church. I wasn't the father you needed me to be. I wasn't there for you when you needed me most. And I didn't take your side. I took my own. There's nothing I can say that will make amends for that, but I just needed you to know that I've regretted that every day since you've been gone. If I could change one thing in my life, it would be that moment. I am so sorry, Hannah."

"Please don't call me that," I said quietly. His brows knitted together in confusion. "I've been Anna since I left home."

"Anna," he said simply, testing it out.

"I don't think I can forgive you yet," I admitted. "But maybe we can get there in time," I said, and I noticed he visibly sighed in relief at my words.

"Can I give you a hug, Anna?" he asked tentatively. I thought about it for ten seconds or so before reluctantly nodding. I stood carefully, still mindful of my injuries. He walked up to me slowly, giving me time to change my mind. When he was close, he opened his arms and waited, letting me make this decision for myself. I closed the distance between us, and when he folded his arms around me and I took in his familiar scent, I broke down in sobs. I could feel him crying too, but his hold never broke. Suddenly I heard my mother's voice in my head. *He's a changed man.*

When the tears finally subsided, I pulled away. My father had a smile on his handsome face, and warmth in his eyes that I had never seen before. I smiled in return before asking him a question that would immediately test him. There was something that I needed to know before I let him back into my life.

"Dad, want to meet my girlfriend?" His eyebrows rose in surprise before he nodded. I sat back down on the bed and told him to bring Molly back in.

Seconds later, she was at my side. I grabbed her hand tightly in mine, giving her a reassuring look. "Dad, this is my girlfriend, Molly. Molly, this is my dad, Peter.

Molly held out the hand I wasn't holding. "Nice to meet you, Peter."

"It's a pleasure to meet you, Molly," he said with more sincerity than I had ever heard from him. Maybe Mom was right and he had changed. "How long have you and my daughter been an item?"

"About a month and a half now," she replied.

"Do you love her?"

"With all my heart." He smiled broadly.

"As long as you treat her well and you love her, that's all I care about," he said simply. As long as I lived, I never expected to hear those words out of his mouth. "So, tell me about yourself."

I proceeded to tell him about my career, about who I'd become, about Molly and how we met, and finally about us moving in together in Colorado Springs.

"Wow. That's all so great, Anna Banana."

I smiled at his new version of my old nickname.

"So, what's new with you?" I asked.

"Well, we're no longer Jehovah's Witnesses," he told me.

"What?!" I exclaimed. I literally could not believe it. That was the last thing I expected to come out of his mouth.

"Yeah, after you left, I started pulling back. The church got upset with me because I wasn't dedicating enough time to them, even though they knew that I was looking for you. I told them you were my main priority and that I knew that God knew that. They took away my status, and after that I left. It wasn't until then that I realized how toxic our church was." I nodded in complete understanding. "So, now we just go to a nondenominational Christian church. We all like it so much better, and that's where Nathan met his wife."

"Nathan's married?" I asked. He was just shocking me all over the place today.

"He is. He got married three years ago, and they have twin girls."

I was speechless. All these years I assumed that he actually wanted me dead. I never thought he would've moved on with his own life and started a family.

"Wow. Good for him. I know you said he's here, but I'm just not ready to see him yet," I admitted softly. Just hearing his name still gave me the shivers and I didn't know if that would ever change, even if he had.

"I understand. And so does he. He told me he will never push you to meet him. If you never want to, you never have to."

I nodded, grateful that there was no pressure. Suddenly, I felt exhausted. I struggled to keep my eyes open and all I wanted to do was lie down.

"You need to rest. I'll see you soon, okay?" My dad came over and kissed my forehead before leaving a slip of paper with his number on it on the table next to my bed. "I love you, honey. I'm so glad you're safe." I smiled in return, not ready to say the L word to him yet.

I was asleep as soon as my head hit the pillow.

Chapter 22

Molly

Anna was let out of the hospital two days later. I surprised her with a little get-together of her friends waiting at her apartment. She squealed in surprise and excitement at seeing them all. She hadn't seen the girls since her dad came to the hospital, and they wanted all the details. I stood by her side with my hand on her back in silent support. I knew she still hadn't fully processed what happened with him, or the fact that she no longer had to worry about her stepbrother.

Her dad had come to visit her one more time before he, her stepmother, and her stepbrother left to go back home. I knew she was grateful that they didn't live here, so there would be no pressure to see them.

"You know what's weird to me?" Anna asked as she finished up her story. "If Nathan truly wasn't stalking me, or planning to kill me or anything, how come I kept getting the feeling that I was being watched? Do you think I was just being paranoid?"

"I actually have an answer to that question," Savannah immediately replied. "It was Greg. The cops found his cell phone and there were a ton of pictures on there. Of me, of us, hanging out at the shop, walking down the street. Think about it, I bet every time you got that feeling you were with me, right?"

I watched Anna as her brows furrowed in concentration and skepticism, looking back through her memories of those times she got the shivers. Finally, she nodded. "Yeah, I guess you're right. I just always assumed that it was Nathan. Well, that makes me feel a whole hell of a lot better."

"Good. I'm glad that I could alleviate that worry for you," Savannah replied, smiling.

"How are you doing with everything, Savannah?" Anna asked

"I'm okay. I mean, it's hard to believe that I actually killed someone," she said quietly. "Especially Greg. It feels surreal. I don't regret it, and he was a horrible man, but it still gets to me sometimes. I knew him for a long time."

"If you hadn't done it, he would've, baby," Charlie said quietly in her ear, pulling her back against him.

"I know," she said as she gave him a watery smile over her shoulder. "I would do it again. Especially after the damage he caused you, Anna." Her eyes hardened at the thought, all trace of tears gone.

"It isn't easy," Lauren added next to her. "I struggled with it too after that woman tried to kill Phoenix." I turned to her in surprise. I hadn't heard that story.

"I had almost forgotten about that," Anna whispered, shaking her head.

"You'll struggle with it, but eventually you won't think about it as much anymore. It also brought me comfort knowing that she wasn't mentally sound, and that she had a very rough time of it. I could see the relief in her eyes as the light faded from them. I bet it was the same with Greg. Even though he wanted revenge, he clearly wasn't happy with his life."

Savannah nodded gratefully and took Lauren's hand. The two of them shared an experience that no one else in the room did, and they were lucky to have each other to understand what it was like.

"Well, let's change the subject," Lauren said. "This is too much serious talk for me. Molly, have you put your house on the market yet?"

"No, not yet. I was originally going to do that last week, but I didn't want to worry about it with Anna in the hospital. I just spoke with my Realtor though, and we're going to put it up next week. There are a few more things I need to get done before it'll be ready to list."

"That's so exciting! And you guys are going to live here for a while?" Savannah asked, gesturing to Anna's apartment.

"Only for two more months. I'm going to put my notice in to my landlord in the next few days," Anna added. "But I, of course, already started us a Zillow account and we've been looking at some beautiful houses. Hopefully we will find one quickly and won't have to be a burden to her parents for too long." To which I rolled my eyes.

"We will not be a burden to them, siúcra. They are going to be so excited to have us there, especially my mam."

"Oh, that's right," Anna added, mischief gleaming in her eyes. "She'll be thrilled that her new *favorite* daughter is going to be living with them."

"Brat," I retorted, nipping her finger in punishment. Her eyes latched on to my mouth as her gaze grew hot. I knew that look, and she wasn't nearly ready for that yet. I gently put her hand in her own lap before whispering to her, "Behave."

We ordered in Italian food, since Anna requested lots of pasta. We chatted for the next few hours and just enjoyed ourselves and the wonderful company. I could see why Anna loved this group so much. They were really something special and I couldn't wait to get to know them all more.

Chapter 22

A week later, it was time to put my house on the market. Needless to say, I was very nervous. My Realtor had told me to get lost for the day so that she could do showings uninterrupted. Anna decided to distract me, and we made a whole day out of it. First she took me to brunch, and then we got pedicures, holding hands across the gap in the chairs. Then, we decided to see a movie, but neither of us remembered what it was about because we were making out in the back of the theater for most of it. The doctor hadn't cleared her for "physical activity" yet, but we were having fun going back to the basics.

At the end of the day, we went back to the apartment and were eating dinner when my Realtor called me. According to her, I already had two offers on my house, and the rest of the weekend was still booked with showings. She suggested I wait until the end of the day on Sunday to make a decision, since she thought I would get even more offers the next day.

I hung up and immediately felt a weight lift off my chest. My house was going to sell for more than what I asked for. It was a nice feeling, knowing that other people were going to appreciate all the work I put into that little old house. And that they were going to love it as much as I had. As excited as I was for the next part in our journey, I was going to miss it. It was the first house I had owned, and I had put a lot of blood, sweat, and tears into it.

At the end of the next day, I had my answer, and my Realtor had been right. I ended up getting four offers on my house in two days, and I got $20,000 over my asking price. I couldn't believe it. I was thrilled.

When that was taken care of, Molly and I decided to start calling around to locations in the Springs to see if there was anyone hiring.

We each put multiple applications in and had scheduled interviews for the next month, when we were actually living there.

We had also started packing up the apartment. We had most of our nonessential stuff in storage, which was nice, but inconvenient at times when we would need something random and it would already be packed away.

"I can't believe we're actually doing this," I told her one night before bed.

"It does feel sort of surreal, doesn't it?"

"I hope my parents don't end up driving you too crazy," I admitted. It was something I was a little worried about. I already knew they were going to drive me nuts.

"Oh, we'll be fine. They might make me a little annoyed at some point, but that's what parents do, right?" She smiled, actually looking excited about my parents' annoying habits.

"So, are you and the girls doing anything big before we leave in two weeks?" I asked.

"Just the usual. Drink wine, eat shitty delicious food, talk about hot celebrities. You know, our norm." She shrugged. She was putting on a brave face, I could tell. I knew she was excited to move, but I also knew it was going to be very hard for her to leave the girls behind. They were her family. The family that she had chosen for herself when her own wasn't there for her.

"Are you excited to finally meet some of my friends?" I asked. I had been in Denver for a while, but never made any real friends here. Back home, however, I had a few close ones from high school. We had kept in touch over the years, but with the distance we hadn't been able to spend much time together. I was looking forward to reconnecting with them.

"Of course. I can't wait to hear all of your most embarrassing high school stories."

I rolled my eyes at that, my cheeks already heating when a few came to mind. I turned my face from hers so she wouldn't see and inquire further, which I knew she would.

"I love you, Molly." Her soft words had me turning back to her. "Thank you for accepting me just as I am. And for being such a strong comfort and support system. I don't think you know what it means to me." Tears gathered in my eyes.

"I do know, siúcra. I love you too. So much."

"I don't think you do know. Since my mom passed, I felt so alone. I always felt like I had to hide who I truly was, and that no one would ever fully accept me. I was scared to show anyone my past or who I had become. You gave me the courage to open up. You gave me the support to help me finally see that people do love me and will accept me no matter what. Thank you for giving me that." She was crying now too, and I wrapped her in my arms as I showed her just how much I loved her.

Two months later

"Oh my God. I love it!" Anna screamed as we walked into what felt like the millionth house we had looked at.

It had taken longer than we thought it would to find a house. They were either too small, we didn't like the neighborhood, there were structural problems, or they were snatched up before we had the chance to make an offer.

I had a good feeling about this one though. We caught it the first day it was on the market, and according to our Realtor, there weren't any offers yet.

It was located in one of the nicer neighborhoods of downtown Colorado Springs, which meant there were a lot of cool things to do in the vicinity, and it was close to both of our jobs. It was an old Victorian house, but recently, it had been completely gutted and renovated. We had walked through the whole house and loved everything about it. The style reminded me of a lot of the work that I had done on my previous house, and was just my taste.

"Do you want to put an offer down?" I asked Anna, hoping she would say yes.

"Oh, fuck yes!" she exclaimed as our Realtor chuckled.

I turned to her as I asked, "Do you think we should go in over asking?"

"If you are really in love with this house then I would put in maybe five to ten over, but I think you have a really good chance of getting it since there haven't been any offers on it yet."

"Let's do ten over," Anna said. "I really want this house." I nodded in agreement. I loved everything from the exposed brick, to the sliding barn doors. Not to mention that I was so ready to be out of my parents' house, it wasn't even funny.

Anna was being such a good sport, but if my mother gave me another lecture about what she thought we should do in terms of buying a house, I was going to scream. I knew she meant well, but we wanted to do this our way. Plus, the whole house-buying gig was much different today than thirty years ago, when they bought theirs. My da and Anna always tried to stay out of it, usually going out on the porch with drinks when she and I had an argument, and because of that, the two of them had actually gotten really close. I loved my ma, but both of us were very stubborn and did better in separate households.

We left and our Realtor said she would put the offer in and let us know as soon as she heard back. We went back to my parents', equally nervous and excited.

The next morning, she called to let us know that we were under contract. We both squealed and jumped up and down in excitement, and I pulled Anna in for a heated kiss before we left the room.

"What's all the excitement about?" Mam asked when we made it to the kitchen for breakfast.

"Our offer got accepted!" Anna shouted.

"Oh, honey, that's wonderful news. We will have to celebrate tonight when you two get home from work."

When we got back later that evening, Mam had prepared my favorite meal, and Anna's favorite dessert. She also had a bottle of champagne ready for us to break into. I poured us each a glass before turning to Anna.

We clinked our glasses together before I whispered, "To the start of a wonderful new adventure with the love of my life."

Chapter 23

Anna

Six months later...

I looked out over the cliffs and the ocean on the west side of Ireland. The famous cliffs of Moher. I sighed contentedly as I took it all in. A moment later, I felt Molly wrap her arms around me from behind.

"What do you think, siúcra?" she asked softly.

"There are no words," I replied just as quietly, resting my hands on top of hers over my stomach. I didn't want to disturb the peaceful vibe here.

We had finally gone on our couples' trip with the girls. It was amazing spending so much time with them. We of course still visited each other, but I missed them, especially since I had lost my work buddy, Savannah. It had been a hard adjustment not seeing her at work every day. I had gotten a job at Heart of Gold tattoo in Old Colorado City, and I loved it there. I made a new good friend there, luckily. Her name was Liliana and she was super chill. I was already thinking about having her give me a tattoo, and I had done a few piercings for her as well. Molly and I had gotten together with Liliana and her husband before, and while they weren't my old friends, we still had a great time.

Savannah and Charlie were already posing for pictures on the edge of the cliff, while Lauren took their photo. I smiled as I watched them all. Everything finally felt right. I had been talking with my dad more, and it felt good to start mending our relationship. I still hadn't seen Nathan yet, but I was considering going down to see everyone for Christmas.

Molly and I were loving our new house and our jobs. We went to Manitou about every month, and did something new there every time. We also regularly went out with her parents. She and her mam were doing much better now that they weren't living under the same roof anymore.

This was our first real day in Ireland. It was also our first vacation together. We were spending most of it with the girls and their husbands, but we were also taking a day to go and visit Molly's extended family by ourselves. Molly was the one who planned the trip, since she knew the island. She had a few tourist-type things scheduled, but mostly we were getting a local's tour.

After we all took pictures, and also had a stranger take a photo of all of us together on the cliffs, we decided to go to a local pub for lunch. As soon as we sat and had our Guinnesses in front of us, we of course started catching up.

"So, I take it since you're drinking, you haven't had any luck on the baby front?" I asked Savannah.

She gave a sad shake of her head before answering. "No. It sucks. I was always under the impression that as soon as you had unprotected sex that it would immediately happen. Fuckin' health class," she ranted. It was true. Health teachers always made you think that as soon as you had sex, you would get pregnant. Their way of getting high schoolers to remain abstinent, I guess.

"I'm sorry, Savannah. Have you seen a doctor yet?"

"No. Most doctors won't see you until you've been actively trying for a year. I have been doing some research on my own though. My cycles aren't regular, and I don't think they were before I got on birth control either. From what I've read, that's a sign of PCOS."

"What is that?" I asked, feeling slightly embarrassed that I had never heard of it before. I mean, I was a woman after all.

"It stands for polycystic ovarian syndrome. Each case presents differently. Some women have cysts on their ovaries, and for some, it's more of just a hormone condition where they either produce too much testosterone or not enough estrogen. There are actually like twenty different hormones that can be affected by the condition," she said, rolling her eyes.

"So, do you have symptoms of it?" Lauren asked. The guys seemed to have immersed themselves in a separate conversation as soon as fertility was brought up.

"Well, like I said, my cycles have been really long and irregular. At first I thought it was the switch from getting off birth control, but my cycle hasn't regulated at all. I also have anxiety, which weirdly enough is a symptom, as well as excess body hair, and pretty constant fatigue."

"Is there anything you can do for it?" I asked.

"Acupuncture and supplements help with it," Molly chimed in. Of course she would know about this condition and how to help. "I mean, if you're wanting to go the more natural route. It'll probably take longer than getting on medication, but it's worth a shot. Especially if you can't see the doctors for fertility yet."

Savannah zeroed in on her, totally interested. "You know, I was reading that diet changes also help."

"That's right," Molly agreed, nodding. "PCOS is also an inflammatory condition, so if you cut out foods that cause inflammation, it's supposed to make a big difference."

"What foods do that?" I asked.

"Well, for starters you want to stay away from processed shit and fast food as much as possible. You would also want to completely cut out alcohol, sugar, dairy, and gluten."

"Oh God," Savannah moaned. "All of my favorite things," she whined. I didn't blame her. That sounded horrible.

"But, before you do all of that, I would go in and get an ultrasound to see if you have it, then you'll know if you're going in the right direction, and if all that doesn't work then you'll know that you already have it and can try medication once the doctors give you the go-ahead," Molly added.

Savannah nodded, taking a swig of Guinness before replying. "That's actually a great idea. Thanks for the advice, Molly. I feel a bit better about all this now that I have a plan in place."

After we finished our lunch, we went on a tour of Doolin Cave. It wasn't far from the cliffs, and it was absolutely gorgeous. The stalactite in the cave was absolutely *massive* and they told us all about the history of the caves. It reminded me of Cave of the Winds back home, and I smiled as I squeezed Molly's hand. We loved caves, so I was glad that she added this to our itinerary.

When the tour was finished, we spent some time in the gift shop and coffee shop. I bought a mug that was made from the clay in the caves. I mean, how could I not? We also spent some time with the chickens and donkeys outside before we went back to our Airbnb for the night. We had rented a pretty large house since there were six of us. Each couple had their own space and bathroom, and there was a nice, big kitchen.

After taking a nap and freshening back up, we kept each other company while Phoenix made us dinner. We talked, drank, and laughed all evening. We also went over the plans for the next few days. The guys wanted to go fishing at some point, which freed up a day for the girls to take a spa trip.

We also had plans to go see Killarney National Park and Muckross

House and Gardens. Apparently, it was a must-see while in Ireland. One of the things I was most excited about, though, was the Aran Islands. They were supposed to have an old-timey feel to it, and everyone spoke Gaelic. We of course were going to visit lots of castles and more spots along the coast. Needless to say, it was going to be a packed trip.

"Well, it sounds like we should rest up. We're going to have a busy week," Charlie said when we had finished dinner.

"I didn't put too much stuff on the itinerary, did I?" Molly asked nervously.

"Not at all!" Lauren and Savannah said at the same time.

"Okay good. I just really want you guys to get the full Ireland experience."

"And that's why we let you be in charge of everything," Nix added, giving her a rare smile.

She smiled back at him, and soon we were all going off to our separate rooms for bed.

After we got ready for bed and were climbing in between the sheets, we heard a moan come through the walls, followed by a stifled giggle. Oh God. Someone was having sex. I looked over at Molly to find a blush on her face, and a look that said she was about to bust out laughing.

Then, a male groan sounded from a separate part of the house. Jesus. It seemed everyone was getting it on except for us. That would never do.

This time when I looked at Molly, she looked slightly turned on. Her nipples were pebbled under her shirt and her flush had spread from her cheeks to her chest.

"Is this getting you excited, my love?" I purred in her ear.

"A little. It's almost like we're having an orgy or something," she whispered, her voice rough.

"And do you think we should let them win? I think we need to be louder than all of them." I dragged my lips down the side of her neck, nibbling as I went. She moaned, tipping her head to the side to give me better access. I slid my finger along her shoulder, knocking the strap of her tank top off and exposing her breast. I circled the tip of it before continuing farther south. When I met wet flesh and heard her sharp intake of breath, I knew I found what I was looking for. I pushed her back against the bed before bending to take one hot nipple into my mouth. She cried out loudly at the contact and I smiled against her skin. We were so going to win this contest. I heard a bed creaking from somewhere else in the house, and picked up my pace.

I crushed my lips to Molly's. She met my enthusiasm with just as much of her own, wrapping her arms around me and pulling me so I was straddling her. She made quick work of taking off my clothes, and soon I was riding her face. Within minutes, I screamed out my orgasm, and she was moaning against my pussy.

"I want to feel that slick cunt against mine," she said, nipping my inner thigh. I did as she requested, and soon our own bed was rocking. Even though I'd just had an orgasm, I built again quickly, and Molly seemed like she was just as close to coming as I was. I squeezed her nipples as I moved more quickly against her, making her whimper.

"I want to come, Anna. Please, make me come," she begged.

I picked up the pace even more, at this point the whole bed was slamming against the wall repeatedly, but I didn't care. In the back of my head, I could hear the other couples become just as wild, and if it was even possible, Molly became more drenched underneath me.

Finally, I felt her shudder underneath me, and I let go, my own orgasm crashing through me. We were both groaning uncontrollably, our bodies shaking against one another.

When our heartbeats calmed, I lay down beside her and pulled her into my arms. Somewhere, we still heard a couple going to town. I bet it was Lauren and Nix. Those two were freaky as fuck and always took their time.

"Well, that was sure exciting," Molly finally said, making me laugh.

"Yes it was. Do you think we won?"

"Most definitely," she murmured sleepily. Within minutes, she was drifting off in my arms, and all I could think about was how lucky I was.

"I love you so much," I whispered before slipping into a peaceful sleep.

Chapter 24

Molly

When we made our way down to the kitchen the next morning, everyone was already up, although it looked like they had just gotten there, with the exception of the guys, who both looked chipper and well caffeinated. Nix was at the stove again, making breakfast for everyone, and Lauren was sitting on the counter next to the stove, drinking coffee and keeping him company.

"We totally won last night, just so everybody is on the same page," Anna said as she poured us some tea.

"Excuse me?" Savannah said, outraged.

"Oh please," said Lauren, rolling her eyes.

The guys both looked like they wanted no part of the conversation, and I just sat back and watched, laughing quietly.

"We were in it for the long haul. We were just getting into it when both of you guys were finished," Lauren said smugly. Nix puffed up his chest slightly at that.

The argument continued until he put down food in front of everybody, at which point there was no room to talk because everyone's mouths were full.

"So, what's on the agenda today?" Savannah asked.

"We're going to Portumna Castle. They open at ten, so we can all get ready and head that way whenever you guys want," I said. I had planned everything on this trip, but I didn't put times on anything. I didn't want it to feel too strict and too scheduled.

We all went our separate ways to get ready. I showered first and Anna followed. We knew that if we showered together, we would take much longer. While she was occupied, I got dressed and put something rather important in my pocket that I would need for our excursion later. I took a deep breath to calm my racing heart before continuing to get ready.

Half an hour later, we all piled into our huge rental car. I always drove, much to the guys' chagrin, because I was the only one who knew how to drive in Ireland, not to mention I had been everywhere we were going. Nix, however, was the world's biggest back seat driver, and I was about to punch him in the face.

After the fourth time he told me to do something, I finally spoke up.

"Nix, I swear to God, if you're going to do this the whole trip, I will lock you in the goddamn trunk every time we have to drive somewhere. Okay?" He glowered at me as he shut his mouth and sat back in his seat. Lauren, however, howled with laughter next to him.

"Well, you deserve it. How many times have I told you to quit telling me how to drive?" Lauren said as he turned his glare to her.

Luckily, we got there without another word from you know who. As we pulled up, I heard exclamations from everyone in the car. I had been here before, but it still took my breath away.

We made our way through the castle, of course taking pictures of everything. It was so magical. Every time I came here, I always felt like I was in the 1800s. I got more and more nervous as we made our way through, but I tried to calm down and enjoy the castle.

When we reached the gardens, I found a particularly lovely spot.

I stopped in front of it, pulling Anna slightly back from everyone. Luckily, there was a gap in the crowd, so we had privacy. I gave her a soft kiss before looking into her eyes.

"Do you love me?" I asked her.

"You know I do," she answered immediately.

"Then will you do something for me?"

"Anything." At that, I got down on one knee in front of her. She gasped and tears were gathering in her eyes.

"I've waited my whole life for you, and now that I've found you, I don't ever want to be apart from you. Will you do me the honor of becoming my wife?" Tears were now freely flowing down both of our cheeks as I held out the ring I'd gotten her months ago in preparation for this moment.

"You bitch," she sobbed. My brows furrowed. Definitely not the reaction I was expecting. She joined me on the ground. "I was going to propose to you on this trip," she said, holding out the ring she had gotten for me. I laughed loudly between my tears.

"So is that a yes?" I asked.

"Yes!" she exclaimed. We put the rings on each other's fingers as our friends clapped for us.

"Come over here so we can see the rings!" Lauren yelled.

"I got that whole thing on camera, by the way," Savannah added, for which I was very grateful. It would be special to be able to see that moment again.

Anna showed off her ring first. It was a rose-gold band with a pear-shaped salt-and-pepper diamond. There were three little diamonds on each side, clustered together in a little triangle.

I couldn't stop staring at mine. It was also rose gold, but the band itself was braided and the only stone was a raw rose quartz. It was simple, which I liked, and I loved the braid, and the fact that the stone was raw.

As we drove back to the Airbnb, Anna kept looking between me and her ring, beaming with each glance.

"So, how and when were you going to propose?" I'd been dying to know.

"I honestly don't know. I didn't have anything planned. I was just going to carry the ring around until it felt right."

"That is totally something you'd do."

"Well, I didn't even know what you had planned for the trip so how could I plan something romantic? Also, you should be glad I didn't plan anything. My idea when Charlie proposed to Savannah was to have him lying naked on a bed of rose petals."

"True story," Charlie added from the back seat.

"I still have no objection to that," Savannah added.

When we were alone in our room, I closed the door and took her in my arms.

"I can't believe you're going to be my wife," I whispered, tears threatening again.

"Can I take your last name? I haven't felt right using mine, Ellis, for a long time. It's southern and religious. Two things that absolutely do not suit me."

"I would be honored, siúcra."

Epilogue

Anna

A year and a half later...

"Bitch, where's my mimosa?" I shouted at Lauren.

"It's right here, Majesty," she mocked, handing me a glass. It was the day of my wedding, and we decided to all get ready at our new house. Molly and her bridesmaids were in a separate section of the house. It was big enough that we didn't have to worry about running into each other, especially since they would be leaving before us. We had our hair done first and Molly's party had their makeup done first, and then we switched. It worked out really well.

Of course, Savannah and Lauren volunteered Charlie and Nix for setup, much to their dismay, so luckily we didn't need to worry about any of that. I set them up with a map of where everything needed to go, plus they knew they could call me with any questions.

We were getting married in Cave of the Winds. It was one of our favorite places in town, intimate and unique. Molly and I decided early on that we didn't want a big wedding, and it was the perfect venue choice for that.

I wasn't going to have much family there. My dad and stepmom were coming, and he was giving me away. Things had improved drastically between the two of us. Molly and I had gone to visit them multiple times since my hospital visit, and we had even gone to church with them for the Christmas Eve service. It wasn't my cup of tea, but I was glad I had done it. I felt like I was able to get the closure I needed for that portion of my life and not feel so much resentment toward religion in general.

I had also seen Nathan and his wife and kiddos at Christmas. It was very awkward at first, and I was definitely fighting with my anxiety through a lot of it, but by the end, we were talking and laughing like when we first met, and he took me aside and gave me a heartfelt apology. Needless to say, there were lots of tears on both ends. While I had forgiven him, and tolerated his presence, I did not feel comfortable having him at my wedding. It was my special day, and I knew that having him here would cause me much more stress.

I took a drink of my mimosa whenever my makeup artist switched to a new product. I was starting to get slightly nervous, and alcohol was helping, but I had just noticed that I was basically the only one drinking.

Savannah was a given, as she was four months pregnant. She and Charlie had finally gotten lucky. She had been right when she thought she had PCOS, and it took a combination of her getting on medication, and changing her diet completely. She went on an anti-inflammatory diet, cutting out all dairy, gluten, and sugar.

But Lauren took me by surprise. She had a mimosa in her hand, as she had all morning, but I hadn't seen her take one sip. And she was the only one who was refilling the drinks.

"Ladies, let's do a cheers." I gestured with my glass, trying to see if she would take a drink or not. Savannah quickly grabbed her glass of apple juice in a champagne flute. Lauren followed a little slower.

"To a long and happy life!" Savannah said enthusiastically, clinking her glass to mine. Lauren followed suit, lifted the drink to her lips, but did not pour any into her mouth.

"Lauren! Are you pregnant?" I shouted with no finesse. I mean, it's me we're talking about. She blushed furiously, avoiding eye contact. "Oh my God, you totally are!"

"I just found out a couple days ago. I was going to wait until after your wedding to say anything. I didn't want you to feel like I was stealing your thunder."

"I would never feel like that. I'm so happy for you," I exclaimed, giving her a hug.

"We get to be pregnant together," Savannah cried, getting in our hug.

"How are you feeling?" we both asked at the same time.

"Wonderful, awful, all of the above. I'm so happy and so excited, but I'm exhausted and nauseous and my boobs hurt."

"It gets better, don't worry. Except you will be tired for a long ass time. I'm still dead on my feet every single day," Savannah told her.

"Okay, enough about me. This is Anna's day. It's time for dresses," Lauren said.

The girls put on their black velvet dresses with V-necks and flutter sleeves. They had raspberry heels on. We kept their dresses simple because Molly and I had gone a little crazy with ours.

While on Pinterest, I had come across a woman who dyed wedding dresses. I found one on her website that was perfect for me. The dress itself was champagne and had lots of lace. The back portion was flowered lace in a V going down my back and had a beautiful train. It was sleeveless with a sweetheart neckline. The bottom was the real showstopper though. She called it "Phoenix" and that's exactly what it looked like. The bottom was a dark raspberry color, almost red, and it faded up from pink to orange. It was very loud, but so gorgeous and had a long train with exquisite detailing.

Molly wanted to go through the same woman, and all I knew about hers was that it was a green called "Verde." I had my hair swept off and pinned to one side, my curls cascading off my right shoulder, to show off the back of the dress. My makeup was equally loud, matching my dress.

Molly's bridesmaids would be in the same dress as mine, but their shoes would match the shade of her dress.

When we were all dressed and ready, we headed to the caves. I took several deep breaths to calm my racing heart. I wished that Molly were with me to put some needles in my ear, but that was silly since we couldn't see each other yet.

Molly walked with both of her parents first, then our bridesmaids, and then me and my dad. He had given me my mother's necklace for today, and I touched it reverently before squeezing his arm.

"You look beautiful, honey. And your mother would be so proud of you," he whispered to me.

I teared up at the words and gave him a grateful smile. "Don't let me fall, Dad."

"Never."

We turned the corner, and as Molly came into view, my breath caught. All my nerves instantly vanished. She looked like an angel. Her red hair was down in loose curls, but she had a huge, gorgeous flower crown with tons of greenery that matched the shade of her dress. It had long sleeves, with ivory lace on top, and chiffon on the bottom portion. From what I could see, she didn't have any sort of train, and I suspected that it was backless. It looked like that type of dress, and I knew she tended to like backless dresses anyway. She did the opposite of me; instead of dyeing the bottom, she dyed the top, and it bled down the dress. The whole effect of hers was very subtle, the green almost barely there. My eyes settled on her face and her smile lit up my world. Everyone disappeared, and it was just the two of us.

I barely registered the words that were spoken, only being able to focus on the fact that she was becoming mine. Instead of a unity candle, we stuck with an Irish feel, and were handfasted.

With our hands tied together, the officiant spoke the words, "I now present to you, Mrs and Mrs O'Malley! You may now kiss the bride." I claimed her lips with everything I felt for her, and our happily ever after truly began.

Author Notes

I hope you enjoyed Anna's story, and the conclusion to the *Fire* series! Please leave me a review if you enjoyed this series!

Sign up for my newsletter for all the newest information on my upcoming books!

http://eepurl.com/hRZzz5

I love hearing from my readers! Find me on...

Instagram: @L.J.Burkhart.author
Pinterest: @LJBurkhartbooks
Email: LJBurkhartbooks@gmail.com

Acknowledgments

Wow! I can't believe I've finished this series. It took me more years than I care to admit, but here we are! There are literally so many people who have helped me on this long, overwhelming, exciting journey, and I will do my best to name every one of you.

Always first, to my husband. Thank you for supporting my dream and having my back. You have been such a tremendous help, and I am such a lucky woman to be able to call myself your wife.

To my mom and sister. Thank you both so much for always accepting me for who I am, and being so involved with my writing. It really is something special when we get together to brainstorm, and I love you both so much.

To Iris. As always, this book, or series rather, would not be the same without you. I appreciate you always going out of your way to look at what I've written and give your input on how I can make something work. I love you, bitch.

To Becca. Thank you for being one of the first people to read this story and stick with me through the whole thing. I really value your friendship.

To Beth, my editor. Thank you so much for the beautiful work you do. Without you my stories would look much worse, and I really appreciate all the hard work you put in. I enjoy reading all the fun comments you leave me and am so glad you stuck with me through this whole series.

To Les, my graphic designer. I am always blown away by how you manage to reach right into my head and put my idea onto paper. I love your work and can't thank you enough for all you do for me.

To my sweet Sheba Girl. Thank you for bringing so much joy to my life. I enjoy your cuddles and love and words can't even express how much you mean to me.

Last but definitely not least, to you, my readers and fans. I am so grateful for each and every one of you. Thank you so much for sticking with me through this series and all of its ups and downs. I hope you enjoyed these three best bitches' stories as much as I've enjoyed writing them. Your support and excitement gives me the motivation to keep writing.

About the Author

L.J. Burkhart is the author of the new novel *Fire & Ink*. She writes contemporary romance and may eventually venture into fantasy. Her latest works are the sequels in the *Fire & Ink* trilogy, *Light Me Up* and *The Fire Inside Me.* L.J. has been a lifelong writer, starting with songs and poetry in the third grade, before eventually moving on to novels in her early twenties. When she isn't coming up with dramatic plot twists and steamy sex scenes, you can find her doing yoga, hanging out with her best bitches, baking, or reading, curled up on the couch with her husband and dog with a big glass of red wine.

You can connect with me on:

- https://www.ljburkhart.com
- https://www.instagram.com/l.j.burkhart.author
- https://www.pinterest.com/ljburkhartbooks

Subscribe to my newsletter:

- http://eepurl.com/hRZzz5

Also by LJ Burkhart

Fire & Ink

Savannah, a feisty tattoo artist with trust issues, has a stained history. Will she be able to open herself up enough to find happiness before her past comes to claim her?

Charlie, a hot fireman, has a burning passion for Savannah. Will he be able to tear down her walls, or will their smoldering relationship turn to ashes before he can save the day?

Light Me Up

After a devastating car accident that leaves her life in ashes, Lauren is struggling to let go of her anger and move on. Can Phoenix reignite her passion and light up her life?